D1624882

MY   588967
                      19.95
Hall   Nov92
Emma Chizzit and the Napa
    nemesis

DATE DUE			

Emma Chizzit and the Napa Nemesis

Also by Mary Bowen Hall

Emma Chizzit and the Queen Anne Killer
Emma Chizzit and the Sacramento Stalker

Emma Chizzit
and the
Napa Nemesis

Mary Bowen Hall

Walker and Company
New York

First published in the United States of America in 1992
by Walker Publishing Company, Inc.

Published simultaneously in Canada by Thomas Allen & Son
Canada, Limited, Markham, Ontario

Library of Congress Cataloging-in-Publication Data
Hall, Mary Bowen.
Emma Chizzit and the Napa nemesis / Mary Bowen Hall.
      p.   cm.
ISBN 0-8027-3211-9
I. Title.
PS3558.A37166E45   1992
813'.54—dc20   91-41735
                      CIP

Printed in the United States of America
2 4 6 8 10 9 7 5 3 1

1

"A ROBERT LOUIS STEVENSON novel discovered after all these years. Gracious! Just imagine how much it must be worth!"

"It's not discovered yet," I pointed out to my friend Frannie Edmundson. Frannie's like a little kid. She always sees the rose-colored, happy-ending version of any situation. "All they've got is some old documents to show it once existed."

"Oh, pooh! Someone will find it."

We'd just settled down in front of the big television set in Frannie's den to watch a special news program—all the latest on the hoo-hah that had begun three weeks ago when someone over in the Napa Valley turned up evidence suggesting a never-published Stevenson novel. Frannie and I grew up together in Napa.

The news cameras showed the usual much-photographed vineyards and wineries, dressed now in their fall colors, while the announcer explained that Stevenson had apparently sold a children's adventure book, *The Silver King*, to a man named Thomas Lake Harris.

Harris was the leader of one of those nineteenth-century Utopian colonies, Fountaingrove, and planned to use his

1

printing press and his international connections to go into the book-publishing business—he'd had the novel set in type and made galley proofs. But the project had come to an abrupt halt. Old Harris got caught providing unorthodox religious counseling to a female member of his colony; he'd left town in a hurry.

I wondered briefly what, if anything, remained of *The Silver King*. Moldering, handwritten pages? They'd more than likely be illegible, but galley proofs might survive in readable form. And maybe more than one set had been struck.

The television now showed an aerial view. White lettering appeared on the screen: SITE OF FOUNTAINGROVE COLONY. The announcer told us that an old horse barn was the only structure remaining. The camera moved in for a close view. We saw an obviously new chain-link fence, a glowering security guard, the faces of onlookers who crowded against the fence. Which just goes to show how ridiculous people can be—who'd file the leavings of a publishing project in a horse barn?

"Gracious!" Frannie said. "I'm glad there's a guard. Those people seem so, I don't know . . . *intense.*"

"How about greedy?"

"Oh, Emma! You shouldn't always be thinking the worst."

Frannie patted her hairdo, glossy brown curls that she pins in place in what used to be called an upsweep hairdo. She lets a little discreet gray show at the temples now. Frannie spends a lot of time and energy on her looks, and manages to look astoundingly young without looking like a silly old lady. She carries a few extra pounds, but that helps rather than hurts the cause.

The television scene switched. We saw another spanking-new chain-link fence, this one surrounding a small cabin, with a park ranger posted to guard duty. ROBERT LOUIS STEVENSON STATE PARK, the white lettering said.

"Here, on the slopes of Mount St. Helena," the announcer informed us, "Highway Twenty-nine wends its way through the mountains north of the Napa Valley. In eighteen-eighty, young Stevenson, almost penniless and seriously ill with tuberculosis, came to this scenic spot with his bride. They stayed rent free in an abandoned bunkhouse that once belonged to the Silverado mine."

"Oh!" Frannie said. "Wasn't that romantic!"

I thought not. The new Mrs. Stevenson must have had her hands full, with a sick husband in that old shack.

The television announcer stood in the cabin's doorway. "No one knows the exact location of the original bunkhouse. This structure is a replica, made from descriptions and an old sketch. Nonetheless, park rangers have found it necessary to take protective measures." The announcer pointed out damage done by treasure seekers: holes chopped in the floor, molding torn from around a window, boards pulled from the bunks.

Stupidity and cupidity, I thought. Always a bad combination.

"Just look at that!" Frannie said. "People have no decency! And no sense—there wouldn't be anything there, that's not the original place. Besides, Stevenson had already sold the book. That man had it."

"Thomas Lake Harris. And you're right, Frannie—there's no way it could have been there."

Frannie gave me one of her looks that said I was always underestimating her. "Of course I'm right."

Her expression changed. She turned toward me, her brown eyes sparkling, her plump face glowing with enthusiasm. "That book manuscript—what if *we* found it? Oh, Emma! I know we can."

"Frannie, think how many people are looking for Stevenson's book. No one has found it."

"But they're looking in all the wrong places. You and I could find it."

"Frannie, be reasonable."

"I *am* being reasonable. Aren't we smarter than all those people who were tearing up Stevenson's cabin?"

"But professional treasure hunters already—"

"And look at what you do for a living. You're in old buildings all the time, clearing them out. You know about all the nooks and crannies where people hide things."

I should have just said no, but my mind went back to the Napa Valley of my girlhood, four . . . no, five . . . decades ago. Some of the old buildings were still there, and a scant few of them were still untouched. I thought about Calistoga Road and Mark West Springs Road, the route through the mountains to the Fountaingrove site, where there were plenty of old ranch houses and storage sheds.

There's a certain smell that permeates storage places left long undisturbed. It's a wonderful amalgam of old paper and cloth, mildew and dust, disused leather and ancient upholstery. Just a whiff fills me with anticipation, convinces me I'm about to find some long-forgotten treasure: an heirloom, a collectible—in any event, something mysterious or intriguing. I'm hooked on that smell. It's one reason I'm in the part-time salvage business, the other reason being the minuscule size of my Social Security check.

I didn't share Frannie's optimism about finding the lost novel. But searching for it might be fun, assuming we didn't get trampled. Take a shovel to dirt in any backyard in the Napa Valley these days, I thought, and you'd take your life in your hands.

"I suppose we could look."

"I just suppose we could!" Frannie made little sashaying motions, wriggling her plump body on the sofa as if she were in a sit-down square dance. "Gracious!" she exclaimed happily. "If we find the lost novel, think how rich we'll be!"

Frannie's a wealthy widow; she has more money than she can use. I'm the one with no money—I live above her garage in what used to be the chauffeur's apartment, and do garden work and odd chores because she won't take any rent.

"Look!" Frannie said. "It's the place where they found those old letters that said there was a lost book."

We saw a view of a small, tile-roofed building. SILVERADO MUSEUM, according to the on-screen lettering. The scene shifted; inside, three men and a silver-haired woman sat at a conference table. The announcer introduced the men as experts on literary rights, the woman as the museum's curator.

She explained the succession of rights to Stevenson's material. "His stepson, Lloyd Osbourne, was the first inheritor of the literary estate, followed by Lloyd's son, Alan Osbourne. He was a naval architect, you know. And Alan was followed by a niece, who—"

"Irrelevant." This from one of the men. "Stevenson sold the book outright. The inheritors have no interest."

Another expert spoke up. "The thing to ask here is if the novel belonged to Harris as an individual. Otherwise, it belonged to the Fountaingrove colony."

"That question, too, is irrelevant," interjected the third man. "Harris didn't leave any heirs, at least"—he took time out for a smirk—"no heirs we know of. And the Fountaingrove colony, although it prospered for many years after Harris's departure, eventually disbanded. There's nothing left of its papers or possessions. I see a clear parallel to maritime law. The rights to the novel might be regarded as salvage, available to whoever finds it and, shall we say, brings it in to port."

"You see?" Frannie said triumphantly. "Salvage! You're a salvage expert, Emma."

I call my business A-1 Salvage. I suppressed a smile—Frannie doesn't usually say anything approving about how I earn money.

I began to give serious thought to how much *The Silver King* might be worth. I had no real idea, but I was certain whoever found it would be laying hands on millions of dollars. Plenty of millions—enough money to make all kinds of trouble.

Frannie was peering at me sideways, a sly smile quirking up the corners of her mouth. "About looking for the book," she said. "We could get Vince Valenti to help."

Trouble already. "No. Absolutely not."

"Why not? He's been a policeman, he knows how to track things down."

"Policeman, yes. Detective, no."

Vince has a bulldog's capacity for staying with a case until he solves it but nothing much to recommend him in the detecting department. In fact, in all departments except honesty and earnestness he's a total klutz—which Frannie always ignores in her matchmaking zeal.

"Frannie, don't use this as an excuse to play Cupid. Aside from the fact that I don't want Old Lonely wrapped around my neck, it's not fair to him."

The little smile remained fixed on her lips. She gazed out the window, resolutely not looking at me.

"Frannie, we've been through this before. First you call him up and tell him I need him, then he comes rushing over all the way from Fairville to Sacramento. If you do it one more time . . ."

"I won't," she said in a small, childish voice. "I promise I won't call him."

She still wasn't looking at me. She'd keep her promise to the letter but eventually find a way around it. I hoped the Stevenson book would be found pronto.

"Well, then," Frannie declared. "I'll get Mike Channing to help."

Mike had recently started squiring Frannie around. He has a one-man public relations business and diamond-in-the-rough manners. He's something of a Broderick Crawford type but given to silk suits and pinkie rings. I don't much care for Mike. Still, better him than Vince. "Fine by me," I told Frannie.

The television program was ending, a recap of the scenes now played on the screen. "And so the hue and cry goes on," the newscaster intoned, "the fiercely competitive search for an incredible treasure, Stevenson's lost novel. Surely, *The Silver King* waits here in the Napa Valley for the lucky person who will find it. Surely, it will be found—in an attic, as part of an uncataloged archive, perhaps even in an old winery."

"Bushwa!" I clicked off the television.

"I know who else can help," Frannie said. "We can start by catching up on the inside story of what's going on with the search. I'll call Vivian Butler."

"Who?"

"You know, she used to be Vivian Holland. She married that insurance man and moved to St. Helena."

Vivian Holland had been the biggest gossip in Napa Valley High School. "Good thinking," I said.

Frannie got out her little phone book, then began dialing. I tuned out her conversation with Vivian—I'd hear all about it the minute she was through—and began planning ways to search for the lost novel. I didn't pay much attention to the chatter until I heard her startled exclamation. "No! The Wulff brothers?"

Now what was that all about?

I hadn't thought about Morrie and Manny Wulff in years. They were twins, a few years older than Frannie and me; there was always a lot of talk about them at Napa Valley High. Manny and Morrie hadn't attended public schools; they'd gone away to fancy private places. The Wulff family was enormously rich, and the Wulff twins were legendary in our high school days. They held for us a Scott Fitzgerald fascination, even though we knew little about them. They were seldom seen around town, except occasionally at Christmas or during summer vacation.

I'd made only one Wulff sighting. I'd spotted the car first, as it slowed for one of the downtown intersections. It was shiny and new, a Plymouth convertible—and red, bright red. The top was down, the canvas sparkling in the summer sun, the white sidewall tires spotless. Behind the wheel was a fair-skinned young man with wavy brown hair and regular features. He was, in the vernacular of the day, *cute*. The convertible quickly turned the corner and was gone from sight; I never knew whether I'd seen Morrie or Manny.

"Um-hum," Frannie said. "Um-hum . . . oh, my! They knew about it before anyone else? Gracious! I wonder how they found out."

The Wulff twins involved in the Stevenson thing? Apparently, and before the fact.

Frannie talked a while longer, then hung up the phone. "We're all set," she announced. "We'll have lunch with Vivian on Wednesday."

"Good." I was glad she hadn't set it up sooner—I'd forgotten to tell her I had to go over to Oakland to bid on a job. Frannie was busy writing the date in her appointment calendar. I decided not to wait for her to get around to telling me about the rest of her conversation with Vivian. "So . . .," I said, speaking in the most nonchalant tones I could muster. "What was all that about the Wulff brothers?"

$\triangledown$

2

THE NEXT DAY, MONDAY, I had to be up and about early.
I had a long drive ahead of me. A Mr. and Mrs. McAdoo,
who had bought a little house in one of the old residential
neighborhoods of Oakland, wanted me to clean it out.

I'd been hired for my historic-preservation *expertise,* the
McAdoos told me—no matter that they didn't seem to have
much of it themselves. They wanted me to undo a bad ren-
ovation that had been inflicted on the house, cart the junk
away, and then go through the place for every original doorknob or cupboard hinge I could find. Being as they wanted
to keep all the findings, I'd have to bid the job high. There'd
be no gravy this time, nothing to salvage and sell.

By seven o'clock I had my Dodge truck on Highway 80
and headed west. Frannie and I live in an older residential
section of Sacramento, near Twenty-second and U streets.
It's convenient; in five minutes I can be on the freeway.
While I was in Oakland, I thought, I might as well make a
stop at Holmes Book Company—Mecca for serious book
collectors in northern California. I'd developed a keen curiosity as to whether Manny or Morrie Wulff had included the
place in their search for Stevenson stuff.

I loafed along in the old truck, taking my time in the sparse early-commute traffic. I had plenty of time, not that I was all that eager to keep my nine o'clock appointment. The McAdoos were going to be a pain. From the fuss they were making and all the times they'd called, you'd think they'd bought the Taj Mahal. But they had a California bungalow—an ordinary, somewhat older, small house. When I was young, California bungalows were as common as grass.

I should have had my mind on strategies for handling the McAdoos. Instead, I kept thinking about the treasure hunt for *The Silver King*—particularly the possible significance of the Wulff's early-on interest in Stevenson.

Last night I'd quizzed Frannie on what Vivian Butler had said about Morrie and Manny going around to antique stores and book dealers. She thought they had been making the rounds separately but couldn't remember. We wound up making a phone call to settle the matter. Vivian said one of them had started first. She didn't know which but promised to find out. Given that Vivian sucked up gossip like a vacuum cleaner, I imagined we'd hear back before long. Maybe before I was home from Oakland.

The McAdoos turned out to be just as wearisome as I'd expected. He was a dapper sort and wore designer workout clothes. She was a bleached blond in mod western wear. He fussed; she gushed. Worse, they were fuzzy about the distinctions between a California bungalow, which was what they'd bought, and a California craftsman, which seemed to be what they thought they had. The craftsman houses came a decade or two earlier; they're fancier, scarcer, and a whole heck of a lot more expensive.

The McAdoos and I had to wait, standing on the weedy little front lawn, for a real estate agent to let us in—the place was still in escrow. As a point of honor, I twice referred to it as a California bungalow; they didn't want to hear me. But the place was a classic bungalow: stucco walls, elephantine columns flanking the front porch, front door plain with three vertical beveled-glass panels.

The real estate agent, a harassed-looking man with graying hair, finally appeared, and joined us for an inspection tour. I enjoyed the back and forth between him and Mrs. McAdoo. He said California bungalow; she said California craftsman. Every time.

I was edgy about making the bid. I'm tall, broad-shouldered, and sort of lantern-jawed, and when I'm wearing my khaki pants and work boots, I look rugged enough to convince folks I've got the necessary physical stamina. But people tend to think because they're hiring a woman—especially an older woman—they don't have to pay a decent wage.

The real estate agent finally took his leave. I managed to strike a deal with the McAdoos that was far more favorable than I'd expected. Maybe my annoyed expression was a good bargaining tactic; I was downright antsy by the time we'd finally gotten to brass tacks. Still, it was noon before I managed to get away.

The Holmes Book Company has been in the same location for decades. It's a cavernous place with a lot of atmosphere, redolent with the fragrance of gently aging pages and bindings. Once inside the door, away from the din and glare of the street, you're in another world. There's everything imaginable; walls and tables are crammed with books, all organized according to category, and there are more books upstairs. I went up to the cash register and asked for the woman I'd dealt with the last time I'd been there, Phyllis Butterfield. She's a nice, solid no-nonsense type, and hadn't tried to give me a line of malarkey about what they paid for old books.

Phyllis was in the back, I was told, still on her lunch break.

No sooner had I mentioned those three little words, *Robert Louis Stevenson*, than Phyllis gave me an incredulous look. "You, too?"

"Looking for the lost novel? No. Well, sort of. I'm checking on someone who might have been in here after Stevenson stuff."

"Treasure seekers! They've been all over the place. They ask the dumbest questions." She shook her head. "If I could counterfeit some copies of *The Silver King* I'd get rich—except I don't know what I'd put on the pages."

"There'd be some who wouldn't look."

She laughed.

"Think back to before all this hoopla started," I said. "I want to know if someone was in here looking for anything you had relating to Stevenson. Or, more likely, two someones."

Phyllis gave me a quizzical look.

"Two men, a little older than me. They'd look pretty much alike, they're twins. But they wouldn't have been in together, one would have come first."

She looked blank but only for a moment. "Hey—two guys *did* come in." She flashed me a sudden grin. "Wow! If we find those two, do we have a line on *The Silver King*?"

"Not quite. But I'd sure like to figure out how they knew to look for Stevenson stuff before anybody else did. What do you remember about them?"

"Serious collectors, I thought. Both of them."

"What made you think so?"

"The questions they asked. Especially the first one; he really knew his stuff."

Manny or Morrie? I wondered. "I hope you can remember his name."

"No. But they both left their cards. I keep names of people who come in and want something specific." She got up and led us back to the checkout counter in the main part of the store. "We file the cards according to what they're looking for, but this is going to be tough." She reached under the counter and withdrew a thick wad of business cards. "The Stevenson file. We'll have to go through until we find two names alike."

"Look toward the bottom of the stack. For Wulff, Manny

Wulff and Morrie Wulff." But those were probably nick-names; I hadn't ever thought about that. "Or something similar," I added.

She riffled through the stack. "Got it. Two Wulffs."

"Manny and Morrie?"

She made a grimace. "Manfred and Maurice."

If the kids at Napa Valley High had only known. "Which one came in first?"

"The one who was a little heavier than the other, more casually dressed." She looked at the two business cards, shrugged and shook her head. "But I can't tell you which of the cards was his."

I thanked her and was headed out the door when she called me back.

"The first one, he was interested in ephemera. You know, stray papers and pamphlets."

I knew. The sort of thing people tend to throw away: old real estate brochures, advertising materials, railroad schedules, the early-day highway guides. Some of it's worth a bundle.

"We don't carry ephemera," Phyllis said. "I sent him over to a place in San Francisco that does."

"Where's that?"

"The Argonaut. It's on Post Street."

"Thanks," I told her. "You're a peach."

It was still early in the afternoon but, after some debate, I decided not to go over the Bay Bridge to San Francisco. On the way back, I'd be in a slow-moving traffic snarl for hours. I could follow up another day at the Argonaut. Besides, Vivian could probably provide the answer to the riddle: Which came first, Manfred or Maurice?

On the way home, having given the matter some thought, I decided Manfred probably preceded Maurice. I came to that conclusion mainly because of what I knew about Manny's and Morrie's eighteenth birthday party.

I should have made the connection last night, after Frannie and I had talked to Vivian. The Wulffs' birthday shindig had been the focus of gossip for weeks. The whole town had been privy to the details of what was planned—Mrs. Wulff's phone calls to make arrangements having duly been reported to the local grapevine via our telephone operator.

Everyone knew why Mrs. Wulff had married into the family; she was considered nouveau riche at its worst, stuffy and pretentious. And community discussion raged about the event, as she made calls to a man who hired musicians, to caterers, to a professional decorator, to a florist in San Francisco.

The guest list didn't include any of us local, ordinary folk. At least, that's what was deduced—nobody we knew was acquainted with anybody who had been invited. Local gossip concluded this would be a rich-kids-only event, probably restricted even further to those families Mrs. Wulff wanted to impress. But just as the super-swanky bash was getting under way, it was discovered that someone had put yellow Jell-O in all the toilets.

Manny, it turned out.

No one knew how he'd pulled his Jell-O caper, gotten the stuff to set up firm without anyone knowing. The feat was greatly admired among the local young men—Morrie Wulff not included, we understood. He was said to be as stuck-up as Mrs. Wulff.

On one hand, you could consider Manny just plain mean for spoiling the party. On the other hand, maybe he was rebelling against all that social climbing. The point was, Manny was the one who'd done it. And, of course, Mrs. Wulff—and Morrie—had considered the party ruined.

I sifted further through my memory for corroborating evidence that Manny was the instigator type. He had signed up for the navy right after Pearl Harbor—the very day after. I'd never heard anything similar about Morrie. Definitely, Manny was the one who did things, devil take the hindmost. I rather admired him for it. And my bet was that he was the one who was playing the role of Sherlock in "The Strange Case of the Missing Manuscript."

When I pulled into our driveway, I saw Mike Channing's big Mercury Grand Marquis parked under the porte cochere.

Almost immediately, Frannie appeared at her side door. She was bubbling in her eagerness to share news, and *hoo-hooed* at me the minute I stepped out of my truck.

I had been right about two things. Vivian, her vacuum-cleaner intelligence system operating at full speed, had already called. And the one who'd gotten interested in Stevenson first was Manny.

$\triangledown$

3

MIKE CHANNING'S VOICE EXPLODED from Frannie's den. "Christ on a crutch!"

I could hear the television; Mike was apparently watching a news program.

Frannie put on a properly horrified expression. "Oh, my!" She'd undertaken the domestication of Mike sometime around the third date—particularly the task of getting him to refine his language. As nearly as I could tell, she hadn't made much progress.

"Will you look at that!" Mike bellowed. "Stupid jackasses!"

I went into the den to have a look at what was on the television, Frannie following.

Mike was ensconced in Frannie's recliner. In his stocking feet, I noticed—an expensive-looking pair of dress loafers was neatly aligned on the floor beside the chair.

Mike gestured toward the screen. "Buena Vista Winery— or what's left of it."

I recognized the familiar entry to the old Buena Vista building. It's the oldest winery in the valley, and one of the most photographed.

Mike jerked a thumb at the screen. "Film taken last night."

The huge wooden door of the building was closed; in front of it seethed a pushing, shoving mass of people. The door gave way and the mob surged in.

"They had a movie crew there," Mike explained, "going to shoot scenes for a television series. They'd put up some of those big light towers they use for night shooting. But the minute they turned on the lights, half the idiots in the countryside got into their cars and drove over, figuring someone was about to dig up *The Silver King.* The movie cameraman at least had sense enough to follow the action—great news footage."

The newscast next showed scenes taken later inside the winery. The tasting room was trashed, wine barrels were toppled in the storage room, even the office filing cabinets looked as if they had been ransacked. Stupidity and cupidity in action again.

"Damn fools," Mike grumbled.

Frannie gave him one of her looks. Even *damn* is on her list of words not approved for mixed company. "How about some iced tea?" she asked sweetly. "Wouldn't that be nice?"

"Sure," I said. Mike, again engrossed in the news broadcast, grunted assent.

With the cold drinks, Frannie served up the details of the most recent gossip from Vivian, most of it about the Wulff brothers.

"Good heavens! It's just like *Falcon Crest,*" she exclaimed. "Do you remember? Morrie married that Maxine St. Vincent. You know, the girl from Pasadena, the one whose family had more money than the Wulffs."

"Idiots!" Mike snapped off the television set. He picked up the newspaper, rattling the pages and making a show of ignoring our conversation.

Frannie, ignoring Mike, went on. "So. Here's what Vivian said. Morrie was married to Maxine for about twenty years, but then they got divorced. After that—"

"What's the *Falcon Crest* angle?" I asked.

"Hmmm! Well, I'm coming to the *good* part."

I thought of the joke about the gossip monger: *I wouldn't say anything about her unless it was good—and is this good!* I halfway listened, tuning out the details. The sum of what Frannie had to say was that Morrie had a track record of marital problems, including a recent separation from his young and pretty third wife. She switched to what Manny had been doing and I started listening more carefully—no matter that she'd had nothing to say about Morrie of *Falcon Crest* caliber, at least nothing I could discern.

Despite Manny's hell-bent-for-leather approach to most of life's possibilities, he'd never married—at least, so far as Frannie knew. According to what she'd learned from Vivian, he'd followed one pursuit after another: scuba diving, jazz, polo, Mayan archaeology, yachting. He'd tried running an importing business, too, and apparently soon tired of that. He'd do something until he got the hang of it, she said, and then he'd be bored.

Neither of the Wulff twins helped run the family enterprises, Frannie said. That was all handled by professionals under the terms of their father's will—he'd died last March.

Mike put down his newspaper. "The *Falcon Crest* angle, babe," he prompted.

"Gracious!" Frannie took time out to treat Mike to one of her I-was-just-about-to-come-to-that looks. "Vivian says it's all over town about Morrie's wife. Such a young thing! She used to be Julie McDonald; her family had almost as much money as the Wulffs. Well, she and Manny were seen having lunch together right after the separation."

"Is that all?" I asked.

Frannie put on her best scandalized expression. "Vivian says they were in a very *serious* conversation."

Mike straightened the recliner. "Sweetcakes," he said, putting on his shoes. "I got to go now. Oh—I almost forgot. You want to go to the Wine Institute's annual bash?"

By now Frannie had made a face. She thinks *sweetcakes* is vulgar.

"I got two tickets," Mike said. "Tomorrow night, at the Red Lion Inn."

Frannie shifted facial-expression gears, moving smoothly into neutral. "Well . . ." The hesitation was merely a matter of form—trying to wean Mike away from last-minute invitations.

"It's a major bash. Super splashy." Mike got up and came over to give Frannie a squeeze around the waist. "I want my class lady right there beside me." He gave her another squeeze. "Here's my chance to introduce you to everybody."

Frannie, of course, agreed to go.

She'll always accept an invitation to a posh social occasion. One of the reasons she's attracted to Mike, I think, is that he comes up with invitations like this—fancy expense-account dinners and freebie excursions. Mike's major client is a Japanese company producing sake in California. They've recently built what they call a winery over near Napa, no matter that sake is made from rice. Considering the likelihood for snootiness among the big-time wine and grape growing types, I was surprised Mike had managed to wrangle the invitation.

"Frannie's a big help," Mike confided to me, his arm still around Frannie's waist. "A guy in my line of business gets a big boost, having a gal like Frannie around."

Frannie adroitly freed herself from Mike's arm. "Mike," she said in her sweetest voice. "Maybe you'll help me, too." She gazed up at him, eyelashes aflutter. "Emma and me, I mean."

"How's that, babe?"

"Emma and I are looking for *The Silver King.*"

"Frannie!" Mike looked at her in consternation. "Gimme a break!"

"But we've got this wonderful advantage," Frannie protested.

"What's that?" Mike asked, not sounding a bit mollified.

"Well!" Frannie exclaimed, enjoying her audience. "Emma and I grew up in Napa, you know."

Mike looked unimpressed.

"And Emma understands all the whys and wherefores of old buildings."

Frannie wasn't going to get anywhere with Mike with this line of palaver. "Plus," I put in, "we know about someone who was looking for the Stevenson manuscript before anyone else knew there was one."

Mike looked at me sharply. "No kidding?"

I'd overstated the case. "Well, we know he was after Stevenson stuff since sometime last spring. The logical assumption is that he had some kind of inside knowledge."

"Who?"

"Manny Wulff," I said. "From the old Napa family."

Mike let out a long, low whistle. "Yeah," he said, drawing out the word. "Wulff Enterprises—big in real estate development. The family still owns a hunk of downtown Napa, the retirement place out in the country, too. What's it called?"

"Wine Country Estates."

"Yeah."

"Isn't this exciting?" Frannie exclaimed.

"Damn right, sweetcakes!" Mike pounded a fist into his palm, ignoring Frannie's disapproval of his choice of endearments. "Hot damn!" he added. "With what I got, and what you got . . ." He pounded a fist into his palm again, grinned and favored me with a wink.

A lot of enthusiasm, I thought, for someone who only a short time earlier thought treasure seekers were jackasses.

"You know what?" Mike said to me. "I already been researching Fountaingrove Colony."

That was a surprise. "How come?"

"For Napa Sake Gardens—the Japanese connection."

His public relations account. But I didn't know of any connection.

"Listen up, girls," Mike said. "It's like this."

He launched into an enthusiastic explanation. His Japanese employers, eager to associate the luster of the local wine-making tradition with their product, had asked him to search for any possible connection between the Japanese product and local culture. Mike, after much searching, turned in desperation to historical records.

"And," he said, "get this. When Harris scooted out of town one jump ahead of a tar and feather, the colony was taken over by the second in command. Who was"—Mike pantomimed a brief drumroll—"who was a Jap named Kanaye Nagasawa.

"Oh, my!"

"Yeah. He was some kind of nobleman, a samurai, one of a bunch sent out to learn the ways of the Western world. That was after Commodore Perry sailed into Tokyo harbor and opened up Japan."

I was impressed. Mike, for all his bluster, was a man who did his homework.

"Young Nagasawa never went home," Mike went on. "Instead, while he was still studying in London, he got tangled up with Thomas Lake Harris, self-styled Father and Pivot and Primate and King of the Brotherhood of the New Life."

"Gracious!"

"Well, I don't know if Nagasawa bought into the hokum. Maybe he was just curious to see how the whole thing worked. But the point is, he followed Harris to New York and then to California—he was on deck at the right time when Harris took a powder. Apparently he was assistant manager of the place by then. He took over, at least as far as practical management was concerned, the agricultural stuff. He ran the place clear up until after the turn of the century."

"And they were making wine at Fountaingrove?" I asked.

"You got it. Had a great reputation all over the world. Nagasawa was a hell of a promoter, too. In Japan, he was big-time stuff. They called him the Wine King of California. Fountaingrove was a must-see for every Jap bigwig who came to the States."

"Gracious! Imagine that!"

"I been trying to convince my bosses they could exploit the hell out of this, but so far they haven't given it a tumble."

Mike shook his head. "Now it's an even better ploy. See— *The Silver King* is a kid's book, like *Treasure Island*. It could be published in an international edition, bilingual, English on one side of the page and Japanese on the other."

I watched, fascinated. Mike's enthusiasm transformed him. No cynicism now, no hard exterior. He was waving his arms like a kid; his eyes glowed.

"We could put in a preface about how Stevenson sold it to the man at Fountaingrove, and then Nagasawa took over."

Such a preface would require nimble footwork in the logic department, I thought. Nagasawa hadn't pursued the publishing project.

"The idea has enormous potential," Mike went on. "Like, we could go to all the sister cities. There's a bunch of them, sister cities to Japan. We could donate the book to the local library, or to the local schools maybe—the Japs are big on schools."

"First you have to find the book," I said.

"First I got to convince my bosses." Mike seemed suddenly to have a lot less wind in his sails. "That's a big-ticket item."

"Not if we found the book," Frannie interjected.

"Yeah."

Mike sounded none too optimistic. Neither was I, of course. Despite what we knew about Manny Wulff our chances were mighty slim—and we didn't hold a patent on the information.

"Well then, Mike," Frannie said, "you'll want to have lunch with us on Wednesday."

"What's cooking on Wednesday?"

I couldn't resist. "Lunch."

Mike clapped a hand to his forehead and rolled his eyes in mock anguish.

Frannie, ignoring us both, proceeded with the invitation. "Emma and I are going over to Napa to meet Vivian Butler for lunch. She's an old high school chum—the one who told us Manny Wulff and his brother were looking for Stevenson things."

Mike shrugged. "Why not? Maybe we'll pick up something useful."

After Mike left, Frannie bubbled with enthusiasm. "Isn't this wonderful! Gracious! We can be a detecting team."

Her voice lingered on the phrase; I caught the *detecting team* gleam in her eye.

Double-date detecting. Lord!

$\triangledown$

4

VIVIAN BUTLER CALLED FRANNIE first thing the next morning, and Frannie phoned me immediately to tell me the astounding news: a nude picture of Manny Wulff was on display in an art show near Napa.

"What!" I hollered into the receiver.

"Just what I said." Frannie spoke in deceptively mild tones. I knew she was excited, even if she probably didn't know what to make of this news. She loves intrigue, especially if it's got a scandalous tinge to it.

"Vivian hasn't seen the picture," Frannie went on, "but her sister-in-law has, and swears it's true—I mean, that the picture is Manny. The art show is at that little branch bank at Wine Country Estates."

I was dumbfounded. All the more so because the bank was owned by the Wulff family.

"It's just a pencil sketch," Frannie added. "According to Vivian you can't see all that much. He had his back to the artist."

"How does she know it's Manny Wulff?"

"It looks like him, I suppose." Frannie paused, then giggled. "I mean it looks like his face. Vivian says lots of people who went into the bank recognized him."

To borrow a phrase from Mike, *hot damn!*

"We could go over and see for ourselves," Frannie said enticingly. She was still speaking in calm tones, but she had to be wriggling with excitement—I could almost feel it over the telephone.

I'd been planning to take care of some fall gardening chores today, but there was nothing that couldn't wait. And it was her garden, after all. "Sure," I told her.

"Oooh . . . good!" Frannie exclaimed, all pretense at non-chalance dropped. "We can take the Mercedes. Just give me a minute to get changed—and, oh, yes, what are you going to wear?"

"Slacks and a shirt," I said. The decision's always easy for me. Aside from my work clothes, I've only got a couple of outfits. "Give me a call when you're ready to go."

Frannie was ready in what was, for her, record time, and eager to hand over the keys to the Mercedes. Frannie never drives on the freeway; I do the driving whenever she goes out of town. We had to stop for gas, but in a little over an hour we were at the entrance to Wine Country Estates.

Actually, Wine Country Estates isn't in the Napa Valley proper. Driving over from Sacramento, you come to it sooner; it's next to the highway leading across to Napa from Interstate 80—Jameson Canyon Road. The area is exposed and windy; I never thought it was suited for much besides hay fields and sheep pasture. From here you can see out over the Napa River flats and catch glimpses of the northernmost reaches of San Francisco Bay. But you can't see the wine region, the vineyards and wineries—that stuff is all up-valley from the town of Napa.

The entrance was surrounded by landscaping that was still raw and new. There was a patch of instant, roll-out-the-carpet lawn and a double row of young shade trees not yet as tall as the stakes that supported them but already bent by the prevailing wind. The bank, Valley Savings, was among a cluster of buildings—the development's sales office, a convenience store, a gas station, a minuscule post office, and what looked to be a clubhouse.

The bank parking lot overflowed with cars. Curiosity seekers, I thought. Just like us.

The stuff in the art show was what you'd expect for an amateur exhibit at a retirement community: landscapes done in pastels, watercolors of flowers, photographs of old barns and wineries. Some of it was pretty good; none of it was controversial.

Except the sketch of Manny Wulff.

The little bank was thronged; the room buzzed with comment. People giggled, harrumphed, speculated, and just plain gawked. And Manny Wulff's likeness was indeed there—in all his glory, naked as a jaybird. I tried, unsuccessfully, to match the squarish, older man's face in the sketch with my long-ago recollection of a young man in a red convertible.

Vivian Butler had been right. The way he was posed, in a three-quarter view from the rear, the sketch didn't show all that much. He had one hand on his hip and was grinning over his shoulder with brazen coquettishness. Which made it all the more fun—he was no Jack LaLanne. His physique was all paunch and haunch, sag and bag.

"Gracious!" Frannie breathed.

"I like it," I said. "I like the grin."

The sketch was obviously the work of a professional artist, skillfully designed to make Manny's grin the focal point. Curious as to who had done the work, I peered more closely. It was signed with surprising legibility. Someone named Adrianna Knaupp.

I stood back again, to gain perspective on the picture. I had to admit I was taken by Manny's devil-may-care grin. And his cheek, so to speak.

My thoughts were interrupted by a quavery-voiced old gal who wondered out loud whether the person in the sketch was actually male. "Well, he does sort of have . . . breasts," she commented, to no one in particular. Frannie, standing by my side, nudged me with an elbow. She was doing her best to suppress a smirk.

I gave the woman, who was just in front of us, a closer

inspection. She was one of those white-at-the-roots blonds, with dark brown penciled-on eyebrows and bright lipstick that bled into the crevices above and below her lips. She was little and skinny, thin-shouldered and stooped. She wore a cream-colored jogging suit, which she had carefully coordinated with same-color nylons and patent leather mid-heel pumps.

She was the sort, I thought, who had spent a lifetime trying her hardest and usually missing the mark. I wondered how that would feel; I didn't think I'd like it.

I turned my attention back to the sketch. I surely did admire Manny's grin. Also the *je ne sais* what-the-hell *quoi* attitude that I was certain went with it. He was a product of lifelong wealth, I thought, someone with absolute self-confidence, always assured of getting his way. The grin seemed to say, To hell with you if you don't like the way I look. I'm me and that's good enough for anybody.

I was bumped into from behind, then shoved aside; I nearly lost my balance and fell into Frannie.

"Hey!" I yelled.

The man who'd pushed past ignored me, as well as the other people who were protesting. He'd also knocked the woman in the cream-colored jogging suit to one side; she would have fallen if someone beside her hadn't caught her elbow.

He stood for a moment directly in front of the sketch of Manny, blocking everyone's view of it. He wore jeans, a tight-fitting tie-dyed T-shirt, and a bandanna. He was breathing hard—not from physical exertion, I thought, but from anger. I watched him, fascinated, staring at his muscled back. He breathed in and out in quick, short gasps, his fists clenching and unclenching. He seemed in a towering rage. But why?

He whirled suddenly, brushed past Frannie and me. I caught a glimpse of a swarthy face, the mouth downturned, black, slicked-down sideburns. His heavy brows beetled in a ferocious scowl, his eyes were an incongruous china blue.

"My heavens!" Frannie exclaimed.

A murmer rose up around us: Who did he think he was? Did you ever see the like? People nowadays have no manners.

"Come on, Frannie," I said. "Let's see if we can get his license number."

"What?" Frannie was slow to respond to my urgent tug on her arm. "Oh! My! Yes!" She trailed behind me as I hurried through the crowded lobby and out the door.

We hadn't moved quickly enough. We were only a few steps outside the bank's entrance when I heard a motorcycle engine cough into life.

The man was not ten feet away, head down, concentrating on turning the bike around for a quick getaway. He kicked angrily at the ground, trying to make his turn as fast as possible, then accelerated as he left the parking lot. Bits of gravel made a noisy scatter against the sides of parked cars.

He might as well have saved himself the trouble, I thought. We'd never be able to get to Frannie's car in time to catch up with him, nor even follow quickly enough to see which way the bike turned when he reached Jameson Canyon Road.

By now Frannie had come up beside me. "Gracious! I can't imagine . . ."

I tried to collect my thoughts, to catalog the man's appearance before I forgot any detail. He was a strange-looking man. Not only had he worn a bandanna to cover his hair, his sideburns looked dyed. Or glued on.

And he'd worn a gold hoop in one ear—in recent years I've gotten used to seeing men wearing earrings, but not hoops. His body was hard and muscular, but to my eye he didn't seem young. Also, his complexion was the color of mahogany. But it wasn't the usual suntan, and not that combination of grime and sunburn that marks field workers or down-and-outers. It looked more like stage makeup. In all, the getup made me think of a stage costume for something halfway between *Pirates of Penzance* and *Hair*.

The motorcycle was something else, too. He hadn't left with the expectable roar. The bike had been remarkably quiet—the scatter of gravel hitting nearby cars was the loudest sound I remembered. The motorcycle was black and, unless I missed my guess, an older model. It seemed to me I'd seen the familiar outline of the Harley-Davidson logo, but I wasn't sure.

"Did you get a good look at that man?" I asked Frannie.

"Not really. Gracious! The way he elbowed past everyone, I scarcely saw him."

"Did you see his face at all?"

"Yes. Sort of. A little."

"Do you think that was stage makeup?"

Frannie gave the matter some consideration.

"It could have been," she said. "He certainly did have a peculiar look."

"I can't figure out his appearance," I said. "The nearest label I can put on it is *operetta hippie.*"

We stood in silence, both lost in our own thoughts. Then Frannie stirred restlessly and sighed. "Well, I suppose that's that."

▽

5

"NOTHING MORE WE CAN do here, I guess," I told Frannie.

I wished we'd gotten out of the bank a moment sooner; I might have been able to get the license number on the motorcycle. I felt unaccountably disappointed—not that I'd any idea what to expect when we decided to make the excursion. The surprising appearance of the operetta hippie had put a sudden new twist on events, but now that he was out of sight, the episode was abruptly, disappointingly ended.

At least the picture of Manny Wulff hadn't been a disappointment. I had to smile, remembering the pose. And that grin.

Reluctantly, we both got into Frannie's Mercedes. I didn't start the engine right away.

"You want to go back inside for another look at that sketch?" I asked.

"No. We probably ought to be getting back."

As I was pulling out of the bank parking lot it occurred to me that we were already halfway to San Francisco, within striking distance of The Argonaut. I'd been planning to swing over there after I started work at the McAdoo house, but there was no telling how long it would be before it was out of escrow.

"How would you like to continue the expedition?" I asked Frannie. "We could keep going, on over to San Francisco to that place the clerk at Holmes Book Company told me about—The Argonaut."

Frannie looked at her wristwatch. "I have to be at the beauty parlor at two."

The Wine Institute dinner. I'd forgotten. And I hadn't caught the tone of her voice when she said we had to start back. "First things first," I said resignedly. When we got to Jameson Canyon Road, I turned right, toward Sacramento.

As it turned out, we got back in time to have lunch before Frannie's appointment. Then I changed clothes and went out to work in the garden. The October afternoon was hot; I took it easy. I gave an extra watering to the maidenhair fern that grew on the shady side of the porte cochere and sacked up a couple of bags of fallen magnolia leaves for winter mulch. Then I took the dead blooms off the marigolds out front and the gerbera daisies by the back fence, pulling the occasional weed while I was at it. And all the while two images in my mind clamored for attention—Manny Wulff with his cheeky grin and the operetta hippie with his angry scowl and clenched fists.

Before long I decided to call it a day. I took time to clip a late-season rose, deep red and fragrant, to adorn my kitchen table, then headed up the stairs beside the garage. I'd paused to stand on the little upstairs porch and survey the backyard. The ivy that overgrew the alley fence needed trimming again, I noticed.

My phone rang.

It was Vivian, breathless, apparently with some new piece of gossip.

"Well, you're home, at least. I tried Frannie first, but she's not answering."

"She went to the beauty shop. What's up?"

"My dear, you're just not going to believe this."

After today, I thought, I'd believe anything. "Believe what?"

"Well, my cousin Elizabeth—the one who lives in St. Helena?—her daughter works at World Travel there in town. You know, the place right on the main street. You just can't *imagine* what she told Elizabeth."

I cradled the receiver against my shoulder and went to the sink, trailing the phone cord behind me. "What did she say?"

"Well, maybe it doesn't mean anything at all. I mean, the man *is* given to going off suddenly. Strange behavior and all . . ."

She must be talking about Manny Wulff, I thought. She'd paused for dramatic effect. I got down a glass and filled it with water, then put the rose in the glass and set it on my little kitchen table.

"Strange behavior, I must say," Vivian went on, then paused again. She was waiting for an eager prompt from me. My curiosity overcame my stubborn streak. "Who are you taking about?" I asked obligingly.

"Would you believe it? Manny Wulff!"

"What about him?"

"My dear! Elizabeth's daughter thinks he's gone missing."

First the picture, and now this. "Why does she think he's missing?"

"Well, I told you. Elizabeth's girl works at that travel agency. It's the one Manny Wulff uses all the time."

"So?"

"So he'd ordered tickets for a two-week stay in Oaxaca; he goes every now and then to this resort down there." She paused. *Significant information follows*—I got the cue. "My dear, he never picked up the tickets." *Portentous silence.*

"Maybe he changed his mind about taking the trip," I said.

"Well, that's what Elizabeth's daughter thought at first." I waited.

"But then, you know, with his picture in the bank and all, she started asking questions. The man's secretary has no idea where he is—his lawyer's secretary, that is. That's where people have to leave messages for him. And no one around town has seen hide nor hair of him."

I'd just come back from seeing plenty of his hide but decided not to mention that. "How long ago was he supposed to leave?"

"A week. More, maybe. Oh, dear, I forgot to ask."

"Maybe his brother knows where he is."

"Morrie? I don't know. After all . . ." Another significant pause. "They're not exactly close, what with one thing and another."

I had to dredge around for a minute before I could interpret that. "Right. Manny was seen having lunch with Morrie's wife."

Vivian was primly silent.

"Do you know Manny's lawyer's name?" I asked, wondering whether all of this was really significant enough to warrant checking on Manny's whereabouts.

"No, but Elizabeth does."

Of course. "Does she know how to get in touch with Morrie Wulff?" I asked.

"Well, everyone knows where Morrie lives, on the old Horst estate. But he's a *terribly* private person, you know. There's this big electronic security gate at the beginning of his driveway—you have to have one of those things like a credit card to get in, Elizabeth says—and I don't think he has the same lawyer." Her tone had become disapproving. "He doesn't mingle with the town people, never has. Now I always say—"

"Maybe somebody ought to mingle with him," I put in. "Tell him his brother's missing." And, I thought, ask him what he knows about the rest of it—the sketch at the bank, the weird man who seemed so angry. "All of this is a little strange," I went on. "Maybe if Morrie's not available and Manny doesn't turn up pretty quick, somebody ought to mention it to the police."

"My dear," Vivian said frostily, "I hardly think that's a

matter for anyone outside the family to pursue."

The trouble with gossips, I thought, was that they often were so damn *proper*. "Maybe you're right," I said. No sense picking a fight with Vivian—Frannie and I were scheduled to have lunch with her tomorrow. "It's probably too soon to get worried," I said placatingly. "By the way, when was Manny supposed to get back from that trip?"

"Pretty soon, I should think." Vivian had warmed up somewhat, but there was still a touch of frost in her voice. "I believe Elizabeth had mentioned a two-week trip."

I thanked Vivian for calling and promised to relay the news to Frannie. "See you tomorrow," I said, and hung up.

I sat for a moment, staring at the red rose. I wished I had taken down the phone numbers from the business cards Manny and Morrie had left at Holmes Book Company. It wasn't important, I supposed. I could retrieve the information with a phone call if I really needed it. For now, the best course of action seemed to be to wait and see what happened next. And I was certain Vivian's gossip vacuum would have sucked up any further relevant information by tomorrow's lunch. With a possible connection to the lost Stevenson novel, the Wulff twins presented an attraction for Napa Valley gossip mongers that was even stronger than in the old days.

Not that the original Scott Fitzgerald allure of the Wulffs didn't still hold. But what was the reality behind it? Morrie had been married three times; Manny, apparently, not at all. There'd been no mention of children. Plus there was the possibility of a sleazy triangle—*if* Manny's lunch with Morrie's wife had been correctly interpreted.

I decided I liked better the stuff that fueled our youthful imagination, the glamour and excitement we were certain filled the twins' remote lives. Private schools. Fancy parties. Red convertibles.

$\triangledown$

6

MIKE CHANNING LET OUT a long, low wolf whistle when
he saw the outfit Frannie had picked to wear for our lunch
with Vivian.

I was surprised at her choice of wardrobe myself, an outfit
I hadn't seen before—a tunic top and matching trousers in
a lightweight shimmery material of dark, luminous brown.
It was modest, but the trousers somehow had a harem look,
and the tunic both concealed her girth and played up her
curves.

Frannie blushed prettily.

"Okay, girls. Let's go. Today's the big adventure."

Mike loaded us into his car—a huge boat with square
fenders. The car was a shiny dark red; the deep color reminded me of a candied apple. Once we were under way,
Mike kept up a nonstop conversation, addressing most of
his remarks to me.

"Yes, siree!" he boasted. "That girl of mine sure knows
how to dress."

From my perch in the backseat I could see him reach out
to pat Frannie's knee. "Frannie, she's my class lady," he went
on. "You shoulda seen her at the Wine Institute bash, she

was the hit of the show. Looked like a million bucks. And it's a pleasure to watch her in action."

He let his hand rest lightly on Frannie's knee. She shifted position, moving out of easy range.

"I never seen anyone work a room as good as Frannie does," Mike went on, not missing a beat. "Started at one side and made her way around the whole circuit. Talked to everyone, never got bogged down in the long-winded stuff. Yes, siree! She's high class all the way."

Frannie had always been good with small talk and was a whiz at names. But I couldn't remember that any of her previous romantic interests had recognized or appreciated her social skills.

"What a prize I got," Mike went on, glancing affectionately at Frannie. She had everybody's name down cold—I mean *everybody's!*"

I considered the prospect that this relationship might be more enduring than most. Still, Frannie had a way of saying good night at her front door without letting a man get much more than a peck on the cheek, and Mike didn't seem the type to put up with that for long.

He soon launched into a discussion of the intricacies of status distinctions among wine people. I watched the flat Sacramento Valley landscape slide past, and searched my imagination for ways to link Manny Wulff's early-on interest in Stevenson with the sudden appearance of his nude sketch at Wine Country Estates. I could think of no reasonable connection to the long-lost manuscript. And I puzzled over what to make of the operetta hippie. He was all too obviously a villain type, direct from central casting. Therefore, he raised my too-trite-to-be-true hackles.

"You get what I mean, Emma?" Mike said.

"Sure," I fibbed, not having been paying attention.

"Hell of a way to earn a living. The growers think the vintners are a bunch of egomaniacs, and the vintners think the growers are all yahoos."

"Interesting," I said. With an effort, I put my mind to the

problems of Mike's job. Sake producers undoubtedly occupied bottom spot on the totem pole when it came to prestige among wine producers.

"Status. That's the key to the whole thing," Mike went on. "I got to come up with some way to deliver the snob appeal to the customers. For instance, look at what the Mumm Cuvée people did, sponsoring that Croquet Classic event at Meadowood Resort. Who in hell paid attention to croquet before that? But they set up this tournament, gave it a twenty-five-grand purse. Now Meadowood's got a croquet pro *and* an assistant croquet pro. *That's* the kind of approach you gotta take."

He let a hand drop heavily on Frannie's knee, not giving her a chance to move away.

"That's why we got to find *The Silver King*. Isn't that right, sweetcakes?"

Frannie murmered something halfway between assent and protest. But by the time we got to Wine Country Estates, I noticed, she'd again managed to elude his advances.

Mike was eager to see the sketch of Manny Wulff.

"Gonna see Manny in his original Wulff suit," he joked as we walked into the bank.

I was surprised; there'd been plenty of room in the parking lot and no crowd in the lobby. As it turned out, there was no picture, either.

I approached the nearest teller. "What happened to the picture of Manny Wulff?"

"The sketch of a nude man has been withdrawn from the art show," she said.

Mike came up behind me and leaned on the counter. "Since when?"

The teller treated him to a frosty glance. "Since this morning."

"Who withdrew the picture?" I asked.

"The artist. She phoned this morning, and we took it down immediately, at her request. She said she was sending a messenger to pick it up. He came by a few moments ago."

"Christ on a crutch!" Mike exploded. "Why would she do a thing like that?"

"I certainly don't know, sir." The teller turned away from us and busied herself with a sheaf of checks.

"Christ on a crutch." Mike muttered the words this time, and shepherded us back out the door.

"I guess we shouldn't have been surprised," I said.

"Gracious! I suppose not. It *was* the talk of the town."

"Yeah. And big shots don't like their bare asses displayed for the world to come see."

"Mike!" Frannie glanced hastily around. There was no one nearby who could have overheard.

"It would make sense for someone in the Wulff family to have gotten the picture out of the show," I said. "Morrie, I bet."

"Yes, siree! You got it."

But it was the artist who had called to withdraw the picture. On orders, I supposed.

▽

7

"O<small>H, YEAH, BABE</small>. I forgot to tell you. We got to stop off at Napa Sake Gardens before we go have lunch with your friend."

Frannie treated Mike to a pouty expression. He'd taken her to Napa Sake Gardens before. She hadn't exactly enjoyed her sample of the warm rice wine.

"My boss has been back in Japan on a business trip," Mike explained. "This is my first chance to pitch him on the Fountaingrove connection since this whole Stevenson thing got started."

The sake plant was not far from Wine Country Estates— closer to the southern environs of Napa, but still nowhere near the traditional wine-growing area. The place had a definite Oriental emphasis. From the highway I could see the exotic landscaping, with evergreen shrubbery trimmed in the Japanese style, and even a raked gravel "pond." But the parking lot was surrounded with a newly planted vineyard.

Mike caught my reaction to the incongruous grapevines. "Not my idea," he declared. "You start imitating, you're admitting you got the second-rate stuff."

There were two buildings at Napa Sake Gardens, a visitor

center and the sake plant itself; clouds of steam escaped from it, and as we got out of the car we were greeted by the unmistakable fragrance of rice being cooked—exactly the smell you get when you lift the lid from a pot of rice in your own kitchen.

"First step in sake making," Mike said. "Cook the rice."

He led us toward the visitor center and a set of double doors marked TASTING ROOM. "You see before you the most modern sake plant in the United States," he said, putting on a tour-director voice. "The rice comes from the Sacramento Valley, milled and polished to expose its innermost core." He made a sweeping gesture toward the end of the plant that was emitting steam. "Here we cook the rice, using the scientific process of steam injection."

He had his lines down pat. Once again I had to recognize that Mike, for all his flaws, was a man who did his homework.

"After the rice has finished cooking, the excess heat and moisture are removed, thus preparing it for the next step, the most critical step, when the starch in the rice is converted to sugar. It is at this time that an age-old fermentation process is used, developing sake's many subtle flavors and aromas."

"How long does it take to ferment?" I asked.

"Twenty-five days," Mike said, dropping his tour-guide demeanor. "Then it's filtered, pasteurized, and bottled." He gave me a wink. "Just heat and serve." By now he'd opened the door to the tasting room, and, with a flourish, invited Frannie and me to enter.

The Japanese woman behind the counter immediately began to set up a little lacquer tray with sake cups, chopsticks, and rice balls.

"Not this time, Suzi," Mike told her. "I just got to talk to the boss for a couple of minutes."

A shadow of consternation passed across the woman's face. She made a cautionary gesture. "Not now."

Mike glanced sharply at her, then at a hallway extending

beyond a closed door. Mike turned back toward the woman, glowering. "I'll wait."

He led Frannie and me to a table in the adjoining room, where a row of windows overlooked the sake plant and the gravel pond. In one corner was an oversize video monitor. Mike immediately went to it and turned it on.

He sat with us at the little table, never once looking at the video, while Frannie and I were treated to a canned presentation on the history of sake making. Mike's expression was dark; he drummed his fingertips incessantly on the table. When the video ended, he got up and strode toward the closed hallway door.

The Japanese woman, looking alarmed, hurried to intercept him. He grabbed her by the wrist. "Come on, Suzi, *give*. Why am I being shut out?"

She did the best she could to put on a smile, and used her free hand to gesture toward our table. "You wait."

"The hell I will!"

Mike, his face white with fury, whirled from her and pushed his way through the door to the outside. Frannie looked at me with a helpless expression and shrugged. We got up and hurried to follow. She'd have her hands full, I thought, trying to domesticate Mike.

He was already in the car. We got in, taking the same seats as before.

"Jap bastard!" Mike banged the palm of his hand on the steering wheel. "He's up to something."

He turned on the ignition, slammed the car into gear, and backed precipitously out of his parking spot, the big squarish fenders narrowly missing the car in the adjoining space.

At least Mike's driving cooled down once he joined the Highway 29 traffic. We made our way past the town of Napa and northward through the Napa Valley. We were in the heart of the traditional wine country now, passing vineyards resplendent in autumn color and one winery after another. I counted the tiny picturesque communities with long-familiar names and attendant memories now bypassed by the high

way. Yountville, Oakville, Rutherford. By the time we'd gotten to St. Helena, where the highway becomes the main
street and traffic slows to a crawl, Mike had cooled down to
a near-normal state. Calistoga, where we were having lunch
with Vivian, was another ten miles up the highway, so pros-
pects were looking up for a pleasant lunch. And, in fact, long
before we'd gotten that far, Mike had recovered his good
spirits.

Vivian had asked us to meet her at the New Spain Spa.
There are some half-dozen mineral-bath resorts in
Calistoga. Hot springs are a feature of the area and, with
them, the town's specialty—mud baths. Actually, the mud
is made from volcanic ash, and a mud bath is a rather pleasant thing. I had one once.

I was familiar with some of the old-time spots in
Calistoga, but I'd never been to the New Spain Spa.

"Your friend Vivian's on the right circuit," Mike said as
we pulled into the parking lot. "New Spain's *the* spot among
the valley's elite. No one goes to the old places anymore,
especially for massage. The masseur here is supposed to be
really hot stuff."

"Vivian said the restaurant was very nice," Frannie said.
"Oh! There she is now."

Vivian was waving to us from the restaurant's reception
area. We joined her, and soon the headwaiter was leading us
to our reserved table.

The dining area was arranged in descending terraces over
a steep creekside, each dining space decorated with potted
geraniums in profuse bloom. Native oak and bay laurel trees
had been allowed to remain, serving as picturesque separa-
tors between the terraces.

"Very nice," I commented to Vivian after the introduc-
tions were over.

"Yeah," Mike said. "From what I hear, anybody who's
anybody comes here."

"Yes, that's quite true." Vivian leaned forward conspira-
torially. "This is where Manny Wulff and Julie McDonald

were seen having that lunch together," she confided. "I mean, Julie Wulff." She compressed her lips in disapproval. "Mrs. Morrie Wulff."

"What's new with the search for the Stevenson book?" I asked.

"Oh, my dear. You heard, didn't you, about that mess over at Buena Vista."

"Oh, yes!" Frannie said. "Wasn't it awful!"

Mike changed the subject by announcing that Manny's picture was no longer on display at the bank.

Vivian shrugged that off as no surprise. "Well, one could hardly expect it would be!"

"What do you make of the whole situation?" Mike asked. "You think Manny Wulff really took a powder?"

"Well, if you mean has he gone somewhere to hide out, I wouldn't be surprised." She leaned forward again. "Elizabeth's daughter checked the dates for us on his airline reservations. He was booked through Mexico City to Oaxaca on Monday, October fourteenth. He'd asked for the tickets only a few days before, and they had a time getting them. And he never even picked them up." She leaned back, her disapproval evident. "All that trouble, and he never picked them up—never called, never apologized, not a word."

"Let's see," Mike said. "It was a two-week trip, so he was due to come back on the twenty-eighth. Five days from now, next Monday. Except he didn't go."

"You say somebody checked with his secretary?" I asked Vivian.

"Yes. His lawyer's secretary, actually. Jean Schmidt, she's an old friend."

"Gracious! You didn't say so."

"Jean wouldn't tell just anybody, of course . . ." Again, Vivian leaned forward and lowered her voice. "She's a bit worried. Manny Wulff has been known to go off on short notice, or cancel trips. But usually Jean has some sort of inkling he's going to do it." Vivian leaned back. "This time, no hint. Not one iota. Frankly, I can't understand what's gotten into the man. And that picture at the bank, it's just . . ."

A waiter had come to take our order. There was a lot of fancy nouvelle cuisine stuff on the menu. I decided to play it safe and ordered a turkey and avocado open-face sandwich. The others followed suit.

Frannie and Vivian embarked on a discussion of the soap opera aspects of Manny's life, centering on the peculiarities of men once they reached *a certain age.* Mike caught my attention and then rolled his eyes heavenward. I did my best to ignore him. I've learned, over time, to keep at least half an ear on Frannie's gossip fests. Something useful usually turns up. Sure enough, after a while, they began to talk about the curator at the Silverado Museum.

"We saw her on television," I said. "The white-haired woman."

"Yes, poor dear. The news media have hounded her half to death."

"What's her name?" I asked. I hadn't caught it during the broadcast.

"Chaffee. Ellen McPherson Chaffee. She's a genuine scholar, you know, and really quite an institution locally. It's a shame, the way those reporters give her no peace."

More and more interesting, I thought. "Why are they after her?"

"You know, my dear. It was in the Silverado Museum that those letters were found indicating the existence of *The Silver King.*"

"Yeah," Mike said impatiently. "We know."

Vivian, unperturbed, went on. "Well, Ellen's not about to reveal the identity of the researcher who turned up the evidence. Nor will she tell where those old letters have been sent for verification. People will just have to wait until the material's been authenticated; she's very strong on that."

"Yikes!" Mike said. "The lady is sitting on a powder keg."

Vivian nodded. "Indeed."

Here, I thought, was a fruitful avenue for further investigation—worth every endless minute I'd spent listening to the gossipy patter.

The waiter brought our lunch. Frannie and Vivian's conversation drifted on, adding nothing useful to what we already knew. Mike, as soon as he'd finished eating, excused himself. But moments later, he was back. He plunked himself down at the table, livid with anger.

"I saw 'em. Those three bastards are right here in this restaurant."

"Gracious!" Frannie managed to look shocked at his language and confused at what he'd said at the same time.

"Who's here?" I asked.

"The damn Jap bastards."

"Oh, dear," Vivian said.

"I knew it!" Mike slammed his fist on the table. Plates and glasses bounced. "I knew it the minute he wouldn't see me."

"Knew what?" Frannie managed.

"He's gone behind my back, brought in those two clowns. Shit!"

Vivian threw Frannie a Significant Look. Frannie responded with a lift of the chin. She was sending a clear message: Wait and see. I'll handle this.

"Hell, my boss liked the idea of the Fountaingrove connection right from the start—damned if he'd let me know it. Kept his mouth shut, brought in his own Jap team." Mike slammed the table again. "I *know* those two clowns, I seen 'em before. He brought 'em in over my head to manage the international trade show."

"Who?" Frannie asked, in the dulcet tones of a kindergarten teacher soothing an overwrought child.

"Biff Okada and Slim Takehara, that's who. The Japanese Mutt and Jeff. Okada's from Honolulu. He's a short, fat guy, a loudmouth—used to play football for the University of Hawaii. Takehara's from Tokyo. Tall and skinny. Wears a suit and a damn vest, plays everything by the rule book. But—get this—he always goes by that damn nickname. Chrissake! He pronounces it *Srim.*"

Frannie by this time was making *there, there, now* motions. Vivian looked around to see if anybody she knew had heard Mike's outburst.

"I'll show 'em," Mike growled. "I'll find that manuscript before they're outta the starting gate."

Whatever the outcome of Frannie's project to domesticate Mike, I thought, today's events had brought one advantage: Mike, who had before evidenced only a casual interest in the search for the Stevenson book, was now a fully committed partner in that endeavor. Good enough, I thought. Given enough help from Mike, Frannie might forget about bringing in Vince Valenti.

8

BY UNANIMOUS CONSENT, our next stop was the Silverado Museum.

"Those Jap clowns don't know who they're dealing with," Mike declared as he piloted the big red car back down Highway 29 toward St. Helena. "They don't know the locale. They got to start from square one. Assholes!"

With that, Frannie's chin went up a full inch—no matter that Vivian was not with us to catch the signal. The game I called "The Domestication of Mike" might turn out to be a close match. But I was less interested in how all that might work out than in what Mike knew that would help in the search for *The Silver King*—doing his homework was, after all, one of Mike's strong points.

"Tell me about the Silverado Museum," I said, just to get the conversational ball rolling in the direction I wanted. "Was it named for Stevenson's stay at the old Silverado bunkhouse?"

"Right."

"And while he was there, Thomas Lake Harris supposedly bought the manuscript?"

"Yeah. At the time, Stevenson was on the outs with his

family. They didn't like his romance with Mrs. S.—she was a divorced woman with two kids. So he had this notion about not using his inherited wealth. He was trying to live off his writing. A tough situation. Throw in the tuberculosis on top of that . . . hell." Mike shook his head. "This wasn't your typical honeymoon. He was awful sick about this time, too sick to write. So he just worked on some revisions. The way I see it, his sweet little bride had her hands full trying to keep the household going."

I was astonished at Mike's perceptivity about the woman's side of the situation.

Mike flashed me a look of triumph. "I got this thing scoped. Given the situation, it had to be Mrs. S. who rounded up old Harris and made the deal."

"So, if you work out what she might have been doing, you might uncover some useful leads?"

"You got it, kiddo. It's like writing a movie script. You look at it from all the angles, do the point of view for every one of the characters."

"Gracious!" Frannie said, interest lighting her face. "Have you been a Hollywood scriptwriter?"

Mike shook his head. "Nah! Hung out with some of them, that's all. Hell, no, I wouldn't do that, it's a lousy racket. I wouldn't do it for twice the dough."

I was willing to bet he'd taken at least one run at it. Twice the dough was Mike's kind of motivation.

Mike changed the subject. "Did either of you see the article in the Napa *Register* that kicked off this whole dustup?"

"No," Frannie and I said in unison.

"That's what started the feeding frenzy. The story broke first in the *Register*. Their financial writer did a feature on the Silverado Museum, the angle being how it was a financial asset to the community. There was a sidebar to the story, kind of tongue in cheek, talking about the market value of the museum's holdings, and hinting at evidence the Stevenson manuscript might exist."

"And that started all this?" I was incredulous.

"It was sexy enough. A couple of old letters were found not long before the reporter did the story. That's what the network reporters jumped on."

"So what was in the letters?"

Mike shook his head. "I dunno. The article didn't say. Some kind of mention of the manuscript being sold to Harris."

"All the more reason to talk to the curator at Silverado," I said.

"You got it, toots."

Mike had turned off the highway in downtown St. Helena. Now he pulled in to a parking lot, which apparently served both the St. Helena public library and the Silverado Museum. I recognized the museum building from having seen it on television.

The walls were thick, of stucco with clumsy imperfections added to make it look as if the work had been done in early California days. You see a lot of architecture like this in the southern part of the state; I call the style Neo-Ramona. The structure appeared quite new—in an era when nonprofits were often left begging for funds, the Silverado Museum appeared to be prospering.

Steps led up to a small porch and an entry that was a bit much on the quaint side, with ornamental-iron grillwork doors permanently open, welded to metal attachments set in the porch's concrete. There was more grillwork over the windows.

The entry boasted a heavy wooden door. It was massive, arched at the top and had decorative ironwork hardware. Mike opened it and ushered Frannie and me in.

The museum consisted almost entirely of one large central room filled with memorabilia and exhibits—antique furniture, display cases, paintings, and collections of framed photographs. There was an alcove running across one end, with more display items on the walls, and a few books. At the other end was a door identified as the curator's, leading into a small office, and another door, closed, that I supposed led into a storeroom. A large desk of polished dark wood was positioned near the entryway; it was covered with leaflets and small items for sale.

I recognized the white-haired curator. She was talking on the phone in her office, cradling the receiver with her shoulder and taking notes. Several people strolled aimlessly among the displays. I shrugged them off as merely curious, not heavy-duty treasure seekers.

Frannie headed for the nearest display case, while Mike walked over to stand by the desk, waiting with obvious impatience for the curator to finish her telephone conversation.

"Emma," Frannie called. "Come see."

She was inspecting a glass-topped case in which antique toy soldiers were arranged on a velvety cloth. It was a fine display, rank upon rank of finely wrought miniatures. Companies of cavalry and foot soldiers opposed each other on the uneven folds of the richly colored cloth, some in precise formation, some toppled as if they were battle casualties. Also in the case was a copy of *A Child's Garden of Verses*.

"Isn't that wonderful?" Frannie exclaimed. "It matches the poem. You know, the one about the little boy and the soldiers upon the counterpane."

I paused to admire the workmanship of the tiny soldiers, then moved toward the alcove, my eye caught by a *Silverado Squatters* display on the far wall—an enlarged sketch of the old bunkhouse, along with a copy of the book Stevenson later wrote about the experience of staying there.

A woman stood just inside the alcove entrance, intently studying one of the displays in the area to my right; I almost bumped into her—she appeared as startled as I was. She wore a high-necked, long-sleeved, all-concealing dress, and with it a floppy-brimmed hat and huge dark glasses. A textbook Suspicious Character, I told myself. Or maybe she was just allergic to sunlight.

At the same moment I encountered the woman in the floppy hat, the curator must have gotten off the phone. I heard Mike introducing himself to her. I directed a quick beg-your-pardon at Floppy Hat, and hurried over to listen.

Mike had already gotten down to cases. "Mrs. Chaffee, what exactly was the nature of the evidence discovered here indicating the existence of *The Silver King?*"

"The principal evidence was not discovered here," the curator said wearily. "We have very little archival material, and even less that's not been cataloged. The first item discovered was among unsorted items that recently had been donated to the public library over at Santa Rosa." She spoke as if she'd said all this a hundred times before, but she smiled at me, making a perfunctory acknowledgment of my presence. "The Santa Rosa Library really has quite a lot of materials on local history, you know."

"Yeah. So how did it get here?"

"Because the material was related to Stevenson. The researcher recognized right away what she had and brought it here immediately. She had been working here previously— rather intensively, I might add."

"Who's the researcher?"

"Really, Mr. Channing, I'm not at liberty to say."

"So what did she find?" Mike persisted.

"Actually, she has turned up several pieces of evidence, here and in Santa Rosa. The most convincing and specific of these was a letter from Stevenson to a friend. Well, not a complete letter. RLS had started it—he often did that, and his wife would finish the letter. In this case, the letter remained incomplete."

"Mrs. S. didn't finish it either?"

"No, but she did make reference to the sale of the book."

"What did it say, exactly?" Mike pressed.

The curator—I had been searching my memory for her full name and finally remembered it, Helen McPherson Chaffee— absentmindedly tucked a wisp of silvery hair behind one ear.

"I'm sorry, Mr. Channing, but I cannot give you the exact text."

"Why not?"

She took a deep breath. The woman was terribly weary, I realized.

"I've provided news reporters with all the information I'm going to divulge. I'm sure you've followed the coverage quite intently, judging by your current level of interest."

"Well, look, I'm sorry—"

"So please—don't expect that there's more I'd feel free to tell you."

"Sorry, Mrs. Chaffee. I didn't mean to step on your toes."

Mike had apologized, but he didn't *sound* sorry.

Mrs. Chaffee smiled, a cursory, weary gesture. "As I have told the reporters, I had little chance to examine the documents; they were sent away to be authenticated that very day."

"Where were they sent?"

"I've not revealed that information to news reporters and I'm not going to reveal it to you, Mr. Channing. Once the materials have been authenticated, I will call a press conference and release the information to everyone at the same time. Now, if you will excuse me, I have a great deal of work to do."

She went into her office and closed the door.

Good for her, I thought. Mike had been badgering her unmercifully and deserved to be cut off short—not that I didn't believe what the woman said. She was wise to hold off, not reveal much until the stuff had been authenticated.

"Christ on a crutch," Mike muttered. He gestured impatiently to Frannie and escorted us out of the museum.

Mike was still fuming as he backed out of the parking lot. "She had those documents in her hot little hands." He mimicked the curator's voice. " 'Little chance to examine the documents.' My ass! I don't buy her crap."

"Michael!" Frannie exclaimed.

There wasn't much said on the remainder of the trip home. This was the last time, I vowed to myself, that I'd do any *ensemble* detecting in Mike's company. I sat in the backseat of his huge car, staring out at the Napa Valley landscape and considering what might be gained by a return trip, solo, to the Silverado Museum.

I also wondered if Helen Chaffee had taken adequate measures to protect both herself and the museum's office files. I hoped the iron grillwork over the museum windows was functional as well as ornamental.

$\triangledown$

9

"THIS HARRIS GUY," Mike said. "You got to think of it from his angle."

We'd reconvened that evening at Frannie's house.

"You mean the man who bought *The Silver King?*" she asked.

"Yeah. Thomas Lake Harris. The Primate and King and so forth of the Brotherhood of the New Life."

Mike's mood had lifted since this afternoon—not that he'd lost any of his intensity about finding the lost Stevenson book.

"How do you see it from Harris's perspective?" I asked.

"He's got to think like a businessman, right?"

"Gracious! I thought he was a minister."

"He was. Also a businessman. He had a colony to run; a whole bunch of people lived there. His scam was, he got people to turn their worldly goods over to him, and then he took care of them. The point is, it was a big enterprise—he had to run it like a business."

As I listened to Mike expound, I reflected on the change in him. Before his Japanese boss had gone behind his back to bring in the other two Japanese, Mike's interest in finding

Stevenson's book had been different—more in the nature of Frannie-impressing, a casual showing-off of his talents. Now he was dominating everything, hell bent to find *The Silver King*. Or rather to prove he was the better man.

"Aside from bargain-basement rates," Mike went on, "the reason Harris bought the Stevenson book is because he had a printing press for the Brotherhood's newspaper. He had a bunch of fancy international connections, too. He started the Brotherhood among the society folk in London, transplanted it to New York, where he hung out with the same types, and then made his move to California."

"So far so good," I said. "Not only has our businessman minister got a printing press, he's got connections that will be useful when it comes to selling *The Silver King*."

"Yeah. But what he *hasn't* got is equally important." Mike paused for effect. "Once he has the book set in type, it's obvious what had to happen next."

"What?" Frannie asked eagerly.

"What's he gonna need for a book that he don't need for a newspaper?"

I started to think through the process of book manufacturing.

"Binding," Mike said triumphantly. "He's got to get the damn thing bound."

Of course.

"So he's gonna put the job out for bid—print up some galleys, send them around to get bids."

I was beginning to follow Mike's line of reasoning. I wondered how many binderies were in operation in California back then. At the same time, my attention was caught by a glare of headlights outside the window. Someone had pulled into our driveway—who it might be didn't register until Frannie stood up.

"Oh, dear," she said. "Emma . . . I was going to tell you."

I pulled back the curtain and looked out. The porte cochere light was on, illuminating the unmistakable outlines of Vince Valenti's dusty old Chevy.

"Rats!" I said. With considerable feeling. I glared at Frannie; she made little placating gestures.

"Hey," Mike said. "Don't blame Frannie. I'm the one who called Vince."

I ignored him. "You didn't call Vince," I said to Frannie. "Oh, no! You just told Mike about him."

"Come on, kiddo," Mike said with forced affability. He moved to put an arm across my shoulders; I moved out of the way. "What's the harm? We got a lot of work to do. A man's missing, maybe, and the local cops aren't doing a thing—no sense passing up a chance for help from a pro."

I gave Mike my best glare. He was interested in finding a book, not a man. I let him know I knew it.

Vince was already banging on the door; Frannie hurried to greet him. I tried without success to think of some quick and easy way to avoid what seemed to be inevitable: double-dating detecting.

As soon as Frannie brought Vince inside, she immediately adjourned us to her patio room, which is a jungle of potted ferns, white wicker, and flowered chintz. We'd been in the den. Normally, Frannie and I hang out in there—that's where the television is. Or in the kitchen. But use of the patio room marked this as one step short of a State Occasion—which is about the only time Frannie will use her formal living room.

She'd prepared refreshments. She scurried out to the kitchen and returned with a plate of her gooey Chocolate Delight cookies, and then offered us a choice of coffee or iced tea, bringing everything out on her big silver coffee-service tray. With her best pink linen napkins, I noticed.

I sipped coffee and observed Vince, who sat awkwardly among the pink chintz cushions on the wicker sofa. Old Lonely was the same as ever—earnest, embarrassed, moist-faced, and sweating. He's a solidly built man, long of torso and carrying a few too many pounds—he looks every inch the retired small-town policeman he is. I think he buys most of his clothes at the supermarket or at one of those big discount stores. They're always ill-fitting; he has perennial trouble keeping his shirts tucked into his pants.

No, Vince hadn't changed a bit, I thought as I watched him struggle to keep a cup of coffee balanced on his knee and at the same time deal with the small stack of Chocolate Delights Frannie had urged on him. He alternated between grinning foolishly at me and avoiding my gaze altogether. My feelings at seeing him, I thought, amounted to equal parts Amused Motherly Tolerance and Yikes! Get me out of this!

Mike, of course, had taken over the conversation and was busily explaining to Vince his version of what we'd learned so far. Vince, as soon as he'd finished his encounter with the Chocolate Delights and wiped his hands on his pants, brought out his much-thumbed notebook. He took great care in writing down Manny's and Morrie's names and the dates various things had happened.

Mike had started with the Wulff twins' early-on interest in Stevenson, explained about Manny's picture in the bank and his apparent disappearance, and then started in on his favorite theme, the lost book. I interrupted to fill in a few further details—the mysterious appearance of the operetta hippie, for instance. And all the while Vince scowled and squinted at his notebook, trying to get down the salient facts. He seemed to be concentrating mainly on establishing a sequence of events and getting dates and names.

At one point he asked Mike how Stevenson was spelled. "Does it end with *O-N* or *E-N?*"

"*O-N,*" I quickly said, hoping to distract Vince's attention. Mike, smirking at me, had rolled his eyes heavenward. I felt suddenly protective of Vince. Mike had no right to make fun of him.

Eventually, as the evening seemed about to conclude, Mike began declaring his priorities and giving us our marching orders for the next day.

"I give top billing to the library work," he declared. "We find *The Silver King,* and the rest of it unravels. A check of old city directories for binderies in business in 1880—that's absolute tops. Then, let's see . . . tax records . . . the state archive, maybe."

"Hold on," I said. "The search for Stevenson's book isn't all we're working on. Some of us have different priorities." I had in mind checking with Manny's secretary, maybe trying to find out from Morrie what he and his brother knew about the lost novel early on. And going back for another visit to Silverado Museum—on which occasion I definitely did *not* want Mike's company. There were plenty of other leads to track.

"Come off it, Emma," Mike said brusquely. "It's a waste of time to look for some rich guy who gets himself sketched bare-assed naked and then goes and hides out."

"Michael!" Frannie gave Mike a Reproving Look, then announced she would fetch a yellow pad. "We'll make a list of all the possibilities," she said sweetly, "and then divide up the work we'll do tomorrow."

I was glad she'd offered that. I was beginning to think up more avenues of investigation than I could keep mental track of. And Vince brought up something none of the rest of us had considered. "I can check out your operetta hippie," he said. "A guy's got an old bike like that, there'll be people around who seen it. I could start by checking the Harley dealers, places like that."

I knew an opportunity when I saw it. "That's a great idea, Vince," I said. "I'll go with you."

Vince looked surprised and pleased. Mike didn't care—he planned to go to one of the big libraries and start checking out old city directories. He didn't care what else happened, as long as Frannie stayed home. He'd phone her with names and last known addresses of binderies and she could start calling assessors' offices to locate owners.

"If we get lucky," he said, "there's a warehouse somewhere with old bindery leavings in it—and our galleys."

Frannie had continued to scribble on her yellow pad. "There's something we all forgot," she suddenly announced. At the same time she was reaching for her yellow pages telephone directory. Her eyes sparkled with excitement. "The artist, Adrianna Knaupp—we'll just call her and see if she can tell us anything."

Mike grunted in derision. "You think you're gonna find her in the Sacramento phone book?"

I was about to agree out loud with Mike that the artist probably wouldn't be listed, when Frannie yelped with delight. "Here she is! Adrianna Knaupp. There's a phone number!"

"You're kidding," Mike grumbled.

"Look for yourself," Frannie said triumphantly. "She's under Artists, Fine Arts." Frannie had already started dialing the phone.

"Shit," Mike said. He read from the listing. 'Adrianna Knaupp, Portraits a Specialty.' "

"Oh, no!" Frannie held out the phone.

I could hear the measured syllables of a recorded message.

"The phone's been disconnected," Frannie wailed. "There's no new number."

Adrianna's address hadn't been listed in the yellow pages directory. We cross-checked, looking for her name in the regular listings. There was nothing.

Frannie look enormously crestfallen.

"No problem," Vince said. "I can get it checked out."

He drew his notebook out of his shirt pocket.

'A-D-R-I-A-N-N-A," I said, before Mike could make any wisecracks. "K-N-A-U-P-P."

▽

10

I PHONED VINCE FIRST thing the next morning, feeling only slightly guilty at what I was about to do.

"Vince, I've been thinking. There are a lot of leads to pursue."

He'd greeted me with enormous enthusiasm; now his voice turned guarded. "Uh-huh?"

"Well, it doesn't take two of us to go around to the Harley agencies."

A long pause. "Aw, Emma . . . I was gonna buy you lunch."

"Thank you, Vince. But we can do that another day. I've got a new idea. Today I want to check some other phone books at the library. I thought I might be able to locate that artist."

"I told you I could get the Knaupp address." He was clearly disappointed.

"I know, Vince," I said. I contended with a pang of guilt. "I've got some other stuff to check out, too. And this won't take me long."

Silence.

"You're obviously the best person to go around and talk to the motorcycle people." Last night he'd been itching to do it—it was just the kind of thing he liked.

60

"Yeah," he said tonelessly.

"I'll tell you what, Vince," I responded, feeling sorry for him. "I'll be finished in a couple of hours—by noon, at the latest. Why don't you give me a call then? Maybe we can join forces for the afternoon." Emma, I thought, you do it to yourself.

"Great!" Vince, obviously delighted, was now eager to get started with the Harley dealers.

Twenty minutes later I was at the library reference section, pawing through phone books. Adrianna had a phone number with a Sacramento prefix, I reasoned, but that didn't necessarily mean she lived in Sacramento. People who live outside large cities often set up business numbers with the city calling-area prefix, so their customers won't have to make long-distance calls.

It didn't take long for my hunch to pay off. I'd only checked two other small towns when I found a listing for Adrianna in Clarksburg, which is downriver from Sacramento, on the Yolo County side. I copied down the address, 16 Pioneer Court, and replaced the phone books I'd taken from the shelves.

Just as I'd told Vince, I had one library errand remaining—nothing related to finding Manny Wulff or *The Silver King*. The McAdoos and I were sure to get into it sooner or later over the difference in details between a California bungalow and a California craftsman, and I wanted to avoid a squabble by being able to cite some expertise other than my own memory. I found what I needed in a little book called *Rehab Right*, published years ago by the City of Oakland Planning Department. I copied the necessary pages and, when I was back in my truck, stuffed them in the glove compartment. Then, duty done, I headed home.

The morning was scarcely over; it was only 11:30. Last night I had made a copy of Frannie's list. Now I checked it, wanting to set my own priorities.

Talk to Morrie Wulff. Simple and obvious. The only thing lacking was his phone number, which was unlisted. I kicked myself again for not having copied the information from those two business cards earlier. But that could be remedied. I phoned Holmes Book Company and asked for my friend Phyllis.

It was her day off; she'd be in tomorrow. I thought a moment, and added *Go to Argonaut Books* to my list.

The phone rang.

Vince, of course.

"I checked out all the bike dealers that sell Harleys," he said. "A couple other places, too. Nothing."

"That's too bad."

"I been talking to the Napa cops."

"Oh?"

"Yeah. They got their hands full, what with all the nuts looking for that book."

I could well imagine.

"I picked up something kinda interesting. You know those two Japanese guys that Mike told us about? They got themselves arrested for trespassing over at that Fountaingrove place."

A tidbit of gossip that would give Mike enormous satisfaction, I thought. "Sounds like those two gentlemen are taking their assignment seriously."

"They were dumb to do that. There's nothing there, just the old barn."

"You're right, Vince. Did you learn anything else?"

"I asked the Napa cops, were they gonna look for Manny Wulff."

"And?"

"They knew he never went on that Mexican vacation. But they ain't gonna pursue it—unless and until someone in the family asks 'em to."

Napa was still basically a small town, I thought, even after all these years. "I'm not surprised."

"Yeah. Everybody knows Morrie and Manny Wulff were collecting Stevenson stuff ahead of anybody else—there's lotsa talk about that."

I could well imagine.

"The Napa guys say people been bugging Manny about it something fierce. Morrie, too. The way they read it, maybe Manny's taking the easy way out, laying low so he gets outta being asked a bunch of dumb questions."

It made sense. But somehow not. I tried to think why Manny would have bothered with airline reservations he didn't plan to use.

"I pulled a few strings," Vince announced, his voice full of Pride of Accomplishment. "Got the Napa guys to give me the phone numbers for where you leave messages for Manny and Morrie. Manny's secretary. Morrie's lawyer."

"Have you called?"

"Yeah. They're supposed to call back."

Vince didn't sound optimistic that the calls would be returned. Neither was I. I wondered if the business-card numbers down at Holmes Book Company were the same as the ones he had been given.

"What do you wanna do this afternoon?" Vince asked. "I'm back in Fairville now, came here from Napa. I could come over now and get you."

"No," I said quickly. "I can meet you."

"Where?"

I gave the matter some thought. I wanted very much to check out Adrianna's address, talk to her about the sketch. I was curious to know when and why it had been made, and why she'd entered it in the art show. And who had asked her to withdraw it. Most of all, I was curious to find out if she was still in fact at the Clarksburg address. What with her phone being disconnected I had the sinking feeling she could have moved. However, I didn't want to make the Clarksburg excursion in Vince's company, wishing to make as little as possible of my interest in what he persisted in calling *the picture of the naked man.*

"I've been wanting to go back to that Silverado Museum," I told Vince. "I think there's more to be learned from the curator. Mike sort of rubbed her the wrong way."

Vince snorted. "He rubs lots of people the wrong way."

"Would you like to meet me at the museum—say, around three?"

"Sure," Vince said eagerly. "I can buy you some supper, maybe."

$\triangledown$

11

AT MY REQUEST, VINCE busied himself checking the security at the Silverado Museum while I talked to Helen McPherson Chaffee. He wasn't exactly being unobtrusive about it, but she didn't seem concerned.

"I admire you for your stand," I told her. "Not telling any one person more than you've told another—you must be under an incredible amount of pressure at times."

She sighed. "It never lets up. I have to be very careful."

"I suppose the people who are authenticating the documents must be very edgy about this."

She easily parried my leading question. Her answer sounded well-rehearsed. "The matter will be handled in the strictest confidence, I'm sure."

I tried a different tack. "My friend is a policeman. He's worried that someone might break in here, and go through your office files to find out where the documents were sent."

"I appreciate his concern, but there's no danger of that." She seemed quite certain.

"Why not?"

She gave me an ingenuous smile. "There are no records to find here."

Vince had come over to join us. "You mean you've got them locked up—in a safe deposit box or something?"

"My friend, Officer Valenti," I said. I hoped she wouldn't ask for his I.D. But then, knowing Vince, he might well have managed to retire from the Fairville Police without turning in everything he was supposed to. When he was on the job he never let little things like regulations slow him down.

"Pleased to meet you, Mr. Valenti." Mrs. Chaffee looked at him intently. "I don't think I've seen you before. You're not from the Napa Police, are you? Or the sheriff's department?"

"No, ma'am. Special-duty assignment."

He'd used that line before. I was always astounded that Vince, at heart as honest as the day is long, could so glibly stretch the truth at times like this.

The curator looked at him speculatively. "Well, thank you for looking at our doors and windows. Did you find any problems?"

"No, ma'am. Nobody's gonna get past the bars on the windows. And that wooden door—you got a good deadbolt lock, and the thing's strong enough to stand up to a battering ram."

"That's more or less what the local police said." She was still looking Vince over.

I took a chance. "Actually, this is an unofficial visit," I said. "Vince is doing me a favor." Maybe if I made a revelation, she'd loosen up in return.

"That's really very thoughtful of you."

There was a silence. I waited, hoping she'd say more.

She smiled at Vince. "There truly is no danger, you know."

"I hope so, ma'am. It's not just the after-hours security. You being here alone like this during the daytime, you should be careful."

I thought suddenly of Mike's Japanese Mutt and Jeff. They'd apparently broken in to the old Fountaingrove barn. What else might they do?

"As I told you," Mrs. Chaffee said, "there's no danger—nothing for anyone to wrest away from me."

"Why's that?" I said, doing my best to sound casual.

"Well . . ." Her smile was of the I-can-trust-you variety. "Actually, I have no knowledge of where the documents were sent."

"I'm surprised to hear you say that."

"It all took place rather quickly, you know. The researcher brought the letter into the museum one afternoon. Naturally, we were excited." Her eyes sparkled. "Another RLS letter, however brief, is quite a find."

"I can well imagine," I said.

"What did you do with the letter?" Vince asked.

"As it happened, one of the museum's principal benefactors was here at the time. He offered to pay for the authentication. He took the materials that same day."

She had it in her hot little hands, Mike had said. So this is how it had happened. "You didn't make copies?" I asked.

"Under any other circumstances I would have, but our copying machine happened to be out of order that day."

Vince and I exchanged glances. The coincidence was too much to swallow.

"Oh!" Mrs. Chaffee said. "I know what you're thinking. But it wasn't that way at all."

"You sure you weren't getting a hustle?" Vince asked.

She looked indignant. "Absolutely! The man who was here, the benefactor, is someone I've known for a long time."

"We didn't mean to imply—"

"Why, I've known him for years! And I most certainly can vouch for his integrity."

I accepted that. Her own integrity was obvious.

"I'm sorry," I said. I had something else I wanted to ask her, but we seemed to have painted ourselves into a corner. I decided to try the *Columbo* gambit. I made small talk for a bit longer, then started to bid her good-bye.

"You won't mention our little secret to anyone else, will you?"

I assured her I wouldn't. So did Vince, who again admonished her to be careful. We were almost out the door when I turned back and made my pitch.

"By the way," I said. "I noticed someone here the other day who seemed a bit suspicious. I suppose you're perfectly safe, but I wouldn't want to think . . ."

"Who was that?" the curator asked.

"Well, she was sort of lurking, it seemed to me."

"Oh?"

"A young woman. In dark glasses and a floppy hat."

Mrs. Chaffee laughed, obviously relieved. "There's not a thing to worry about," she said. "That's just Birdie."

"Birdie?"

"Birdie Smith, the poor woman."

I waited.

"No wonder you thought she looks suspicious, the way she covers up. She was burned in an auto accident, you know."

I put on my best *how awful* expression.

"She's terribly scarred. She takes off the hat and glasses sometimes when it's just the two of us in here. I feel so sorry for her."

"Her face is scarred?"

"Her face and arms. It's her forehead that's the worst, and some of her scalp is badly damaged. Poor dear. She's had to wait forever for the damage suit—it's not settled yet."

I didn't know what to make of this. Apparently she had genuine reason for the dark glasses and long sleeves. But Ms. Floppy Hat was guilty of something. I'd bet my bottom dollar on it, considering the way she'd jumped when I'd taken her by surprise.

"When Birdie gets the money from the lawsuit, she'll be able to have plastic surgery. Then she can go back to the life she really wants."

"Oh?"

"She was studying to be an actress; it's what she truly loves."

"She must have a lot of faith in cosmetic surgery." The conversation had veered off in directions I hadn't antici- pated. I felt as if I were losing control of it.

"In the meantime, of course, Birdie's pursuing graduate studies in history. She says she would have wanted a fallback career in any case."

Acting and history seemed a strange combination. But then it suddenly fit. Mrs. Chaffee knew Birdie well. She spent a lot of time at the museum. Doing research, presumably for her graduate work in history.

"Is Birdie the one who turned up the Robert Louis Stevenson letter?" I asked.

Mrs. Chaffee looked chagrined, then compressed her lips. She looked away, gazing at some invisible point on the museum's far wall. "I'm really not at liberty to say," she finally managed.

"I shouldn't have asked," I said. I'd taken unfair advantage of her, and I felt bad about that—although not bad enough to take the edge off the glee I felt at having uncovered this useful piece of information.

I worked my way through a good-bye as courteous as I could manage. Vince and I left.

"Bingo!" I said as soon as were too far away for the curator to hear us. "Paydirt!"

"Yeah. This Birdie character has got to be the researcher."

"Now all we have to do is track her down," I said.

"I dunno. That may be easier said than done, what with a name like Smith. Birdie's probably a nickname."

"But Mrs. Chaffee said she was getting a graduate degree," I pointed out.

"Jeez! Yeah, probably some college around here."

"Sonoma State's the closest."

"We could phone," Vince said. "There's a coffee shop just up the street. They got a pay phone."

I looked at my watch. "It's almost five o'clock. We better get started; the campus offices will be closing pretty quick."

I checked the Sonoma State listings in the telephone directory and read off the number for the history department to Vince, who was waiting, notebook and stubby pencil at the ready. But when I dialed the number, I was greeted with a recorded message. I held out the receiver so Vince could hear. "Too late in the day," I said.

"Bulldog" Valenti, not to be deterred, wanted to go to the campus. "We could ask around, see if anybody knows her."

"Vince, there're thousands of students out there."

"Somebody might know her," he said. But he sounded unconvinced.

"I think the best thing is to wait until tomorrow. We can pay a visit to the history department in person. If Birdie Smith is working toward an advanced degree, she'll certainly be known there."

Enthusiasm lit Vince's face. "Hey, great! I could come over and pick you up first thing in the morning."

"No sense you making the long drive just for that."

"No trouble."

"I'll meet you at the entrance to campus at ten o'clock," I said.

Vince took my elbow and steered me toward the serving area at the rear of the coffee shop. I could see it coming. *Dinner with Vince.*

"We might as well get something to eat," he said.

I'd known all along I wouldn't be able to get out of a social occasion with him. "Well, just a hamburger. It's a little early for me."

Vince slid into the booth opposite me, having a little trouble wedging his girth between the table and the banquette, and looked eagerly around until a waitress brought menus. "Order anything you want," he said. He leaned forward. "Jeez, Emma. This is good, what we found out from that museum lady. We got a lead no one else has."

"Indeed we do."

He grinned at me. And then proceeded to upgrade my dinner order to a cheeseburger with fries. And apple pie for dessert.

$\triangledown$

12

"THE WOMAN YOU'RE TALKING about couldn't be any-body but Myrna Purcell," the secretary at Sonoma State's history department told us. She sounded annoyed. "I don't know why everybody thinks her name is Birdie Smith."

"What!"

"She's Myrna Purcell, I said."

"You said everybody thinks she's named Birdie Smith. What do you mean?"

"Well, you're the second set of people in here to describe Myrna and then say her name is Birdie."

"Who else was in here?"

The secretary, a petite middle-aged woman with a pixie haircut, leaned back in her chair and scrutinized us. I'd sounded pretty urgent, I realized. But Ms. Floppy Hat was right back on my list of Suspicious Characters. There's no reason for a bona fide researcher to use a bogus name.

"No reason not to tell you, I guess. There were two men in here. Japanese. One short and one tall."

Vince nudged me.

"When were they here?" I asked.

"Just a while back. A half-hour, maybe."

When Mrs. Chaffee had inadvertently let me know that "Birdie" was the researcher, no one else had yet gotten the information out of her. I was certain of that. "I wonder how they knew," I said.

"Beg pardon?"

"Oh, nothing, never mind." I thanked her and we left.

"What do you think happened?" Vince asked as soon as we were outside.

I considered the possibilities. "The two Japanese could have gotten the information the same way we did."

"Maybe." He sounded unconvinced.

"But they probably didn't," I conceded. Having let the information slip with me, Mrs. Chaffee would have been on her guard.

Vince brightened. "Maybe they just hung around the museum and followed Birdie. Myrna, whatever."

But they'd known the name, Birdie Smith. "They could have asked questions at the Santa Rosa Library. She probably used the same name there."

Another possibility dawned on me. Maybe they'd roughed up the museum's curator to get the information out of her. "The Silverado Museum opens at noon," I said. "I want to drive by and make sure Mrs. Chaffee is okay."

Vince agreed

We were in luck. Myrna Purcell's address and phone number were in the directory. We immediately phoned her. No answer. The address was in Santa Rosa, so we hurried there, driving separately—Vince in his old Chevy, which is a decommissioned police car, and I in my truck.

The address was in a blighted neighborhood not far from Santa Rosa's downtown. The house was a small, ramshackle two-story Victorian on a small lot, one of a row of houses with peeling paint and front yards truncated by a street-widening project. A rental, I thought, maybe three or four students sharing quarters. There was no sign anyone tended the place. The tiny yard was barren; the front porch sagged.

We climbed the rickety porch steps together. I'd been right

about the shared rental; a card above the doorknob listed three names in addition to Myrna's.

Vince pressed the bell; we heard a loud, unpleasant buzzing inside, but nothing more. He rang four more times before we gave up.

"I dunno," Vince said, trying to peer through a window that faced the front porch. It had a bedsheet draped over it. "Maybe we oughta try gettin' in. She could be in there, conked on the head by those two Jap guys."

"Not likely," I said. "They were arrested for trespassing, not assault. Besides, she was too sneaky to give her right name at the Silverado Museum, so she's not going to open up to these guys."

He looked dubious.

"She's probably on campus," I told Vince, with more confidence than I felt. "Or at a library somewhere, doing what researchers do."

"Yeah." He looked disappointed.

"But I think you're right. She may be in danger, later if not sooner."

"We gotta find her."

"We'll have to come back. Or phone later," I said. "We can't leave a note here for her to call us."

"Yeah. Them two Japs might find it."

We trooped back to the street. I climbed into the truck cab, and Vince leaned into my rolled-down window.

"What's next?"

I gave the matter some thought. "She found that letter at the library here in Santa Rosa. Let's go see if they knew her as Birdie Smith."

But we drew a blank.

"Our history room is staffed by volunteers," the librarian told us. It's open only two afternoons a week, Tuesday and Saturday."

Today was Friday. "I'll check it out," Vince told me. He pulled out his notebook to write down the days. "How about we go over to Clarksburg and check out that artist's address?"

"Okay," I said. I would have much preferred to make the excursion by myself, but could think of no excuse.

Before we headed for Sacramento we drove over to St. Helena and parked across from the Silverado Museum until we saw Mrs. Chaffee show up.

"Safe and sound," I said to Vince, who'd come to sit with me in my truck.

"Let's leave your vehicle in Sacramento," Vince proposed. I agreed, with some reluctance. Having spent a day in the backseat of the big red Grand Marquis as a prisoner of Mike, I was unwilling to surrender my autonomy. But Vince, for all his faults, didn't have Mike's dictatorial propensities.

After we'd dropped off my truck, we drove down to Clarksburg.

It's a sleepy river town, not much to it, and we easily found Pioneer Court, the little street where Adrianna lived. It was less a court than an alley on which several backyard buildings faced. Adrianna's address was the one on the corner, apparently a small stable long since converted to living quarters.

In the tiny front yard were a scattering of verbena and some late-blooming cosmos—also a small wooden sign that bore in flowing letters the inscription KNAUPP.

Vince nodded with satisfaction when he saw the sign.

I pointed out a row of terra-cotta pots planted with geraniums that stood beside the front door. Recently watered geraniums. "Maybe we're in luck," I said.

I knocked on the screen door, which jounced in place. I hadn't made much noise. Silence. Vince rapped loudly on the door frame. More silence.

He peered into the window. "Can't see nothing."

I stepped around to the side of the little house and looked across its backyard. Two uneven rows of pear trees, leaves an autumn yellow, extended toward a house that fronted on the street beyond. There was no fence or any sort of divider between Adrianna's little place and the other house.

I called to Vince. I'll bet her landlord lives there."

We followed the sidewalk around to the house in front. Vince knocked.

The door opened an instant later. A gray-haired woman wearing a housedress and an apron peered out. "Can I help you?"

"We're looking for Adrianna Knaupp," I said.

"I know. You were around back."

The neighborhood eyes and ears.

"Goodness, someone else was looking for her, too, just before she left."

"She's away?"

"Yes." A bright smile transformed the woman's face. "She went to Hawaii, left last week. A vacation, it was a marvelous piece of luck."

"How's that?" Vince asked.

"Poor thing, she deserved it, if anybody ever did. She's a *good* artist, don't get me wrong about that, but poor as a church mouse. And that husband of hers was a no-good. I was glad to see him leave. The stories I could tell you!"

"The trip to Hawaii," I prompted.

"She won it. She could never have afforded to go otherwise."

"How lucky for Adrianna," I said.

"You're friends of Adrianna's?"

"She did some sketches for a lady we work for," I fibbed.

"Yeah," Vince chimed in. "Now the lady wants her again."

"How nice," the woman said. "Oh, by the way, I'm Miriam Voss, her landlady."

Vince and I introduced ourselves.

"Adrianna will be delighted to know the woman you work for wants another picture." She moved quickly to a hall table, and came back with a pad and pencil. "I can take down the name and phone number."

"No need for that," Vince said quickly. "We'll come back when she's home from her trip."

"October twenty-eighth, that's when she'll be back. It's a Monday."

"By the way," I said. "How did she win the Hawaii trip?"

"Well, it was the *luckiest* thing. This funny man came around, selling raffle tickets for his church. Only twenty-five cents a chance for a Hawaiian vacation. The only thing, they were having the drawing that very night."

"Why was that?"

"Some church members had tickets for a package flight, the man told Adrianna, the bargain kind you can't change dates on. At the last minute they couldn't go, so they donated the tickets. Adrianna thought it was a real good deal, and she could leave on short notice. So she splurged and spent five dollars. She really wanted to win those tickets."

Tickets. "Was this a trip for two?"

"Why, no, I don't think so."

A vacation for one didn't sound right to me.

Vince was suspicious, too. "What church did this man come from—someplace around here?"

"Well, now, I don't know. I only know what Adrianna told me. He didn't come here." Mrs. Voss looked perplexed. She wrinkled her forehead. "I suppose that is a little strange."

"I'm sure there's nothing to worry about," I said. "Did you see Adrianna leave for the airport?"

"Elaine Wilson from up the street took her to the airport and saw her off. Elaine and I had coffee afterward."

"Your friend, Mrs. Wilson, saw her board the plane?"

"Yes, indeed. Ask her yourself if you want. She lives right up the street, the two-story house on the corner."

"No need," I said. At least not now.

"We'll check with Adrianna after she gets back," Vince told Mrs. Voss.

"By the way," I said. "You mentioned that someone else was here asking for her."

"That *was* odd. This man came just before Adrianna left. A client, I suppose. He was nice-looking, Scandinavian, I thought, he was blond-haired—you know, that flaxen color. And he was well spoken, too, courteous."

"You talked to him?"

"He came here before he went to Adrianna's. I saw him around the neighborhood talking to people, and then he spent some time looking at Adrianna's house before he knocked on my door. It was strange, but then I thought he must be a potential customer—you don't want to insult a customer. I asked, did he want Adrianna?"

"And did he?"

"Oh, yes. He said he was interested in commissioning a picture. We talked a bit. Like I said, he was a very nice man."

"What makes you say that?"

"You know, you size people up. He was so neat and tidy, that blond hair of his nicely combed. And he had some kind of fancy older car, a big one, very well kept up—a foreign car, I think."

We were developing a rather considerable cast of mysterious characters. Birdie/Myrna aka Ms. Floppy Hat. The operetta hippie. And now this blond man, a supposedly very nice fellow who spent a lot of time snooping before he talked to Adrianna.

"Can you remember anything else about him?"

"He asked about Adrianna's mother, asked about her by name. I was rather surprised—I mean, that he knew it. I told him where she lived. I thought afterward I shouldn't have, except that Elaine—Mrs. Wilson—said she'd heard that Theresa had decided at last to straighten up and fly right."

"Who is Theresa?" Vince asked.

"Adrianna's mother, Theresa Simoni. I shouldn't be talking out of school, really, but it's a shame what she's come to. Some say it started when her husband died, God rest his soul, but if you ask me . . ." She stopped herself momentarily, then went on. "Well, I'm talking too much. I know I should be charitable, give the woman the benefit of the doubt."

About what? I wondered.

"This Theresa Simoni, does she live in Clarksburg?" Vince asked.

A closed expression came over Mrs. Voss's face. "I been talking too much." She moved a half-step back from the doorway. "Like I said, if you want Adrianna to do some work, you leave a message. I'll see she gets it when she comes back."

"No thanks," I said. "We'll wait until she's home."

Mrs. Voss said good-bye and closed the door, but I imagined she was just inside, listening.

We walked back toward Vince's car.

"How about the mother?" he asked

"Next on our list?"

"Seems to me it oughta be."

We looked up the address in the local phone book. The Simoni place was scarcely more than a block from where Adrianna lived.

Vince and I parked across the street. The place had been pretty once, one of those nice 1930s stucco houses with Mediterranean styling. But now the wood trim was sadly in need of paint and the yard looked downright unkempt—the lawn dry and scabrous, the shrubbery anemic. The little front porch was flanked by two ragged Italian cypress that had grown overlarge and encroached on its space.

"I wonder," I said. "The Voss woman seemed to be of two minds about whether to tell us about her."

"Yeah. It's weird. But not as weird as that church raffle. Anybody wants to sell tickets, make a success of a raffle, they go to all the houses in the neighborhood." Vince scowled. "I bet he didn't go nowhere except Adrianna's."

I was certain it was no coincidence Adrianna had won the so-called raffle. "But the tickets must have been legitimate," I said. "The neighbor saw her get on the plane."

"Somebody wanted her out of town," Vince said.

I'd had exactly the same thought.

"So," I said, "someone sends her out of town, and her phone is disconnected. And the people at the bank say she withdrew the sketch from the show."

"Yeah." Vince looked at me reprovingly. "The picture of the naked man."

I was sorry I'd reminded him about it.

"Let's go see what we can see," I said.

Vince took my arm to steer me across the street—after having opened the car door for me. I began trying to think up ways to get out of playing detective duo with him tomorrow.

He rang the doorbell of Theresa Simoni's house; I could hear it chiming inside. We waited, listening to the same no-one-home silence as at Adrianna's.

But it was different here, I thought. There were no homey touches to lighten the forlorn aspect of the neglected little house; no one had seeded the yard with cosmos or watered the dry, dusty plantings.

Vince rang again, then knocked loudly. "We're not gonna get an answer," he announced. He walked over to peer into the front window. "Nothing to see; the drapes are closed up real tight."

He walked around to check the back of the house. While I waited, I noticed at the curb a battered garbage can that lay on its side. It must have been put out and the garbage collected sometime previously. I wondered how long ago.

Vince came back, shaking his head to indicate he'd learned nothing. "I'm getting tired of checking out places where no one's home."

"Me, too," I said.

$\triangledown$

13

I DROVE DOWN TO Clarksburg again the next morning, this time in Frannie's company.

"My, but it's nice to be out," she said.

"Lovely day," I agreed absentmindedly. I had just finished thinking through my plans for tomorrow. I was supposed to meet with the McAdoos again. And this time, because it was the weekend and there'd be no commuter traffic, I'd be able to continue on to San Francisco and see what I could learn at The Argonaut.

"Well, yes, it's lovely autumn weather," Frannie said. "But what I meant was, it's nice to be doing some real out-in-the-world detecting. Gracious! I got so tired of making phone calls yesterday."

"But they paid off," I said.

As much as I hated to admit it, Mike's idea about looking up old binderies showed promise. Two sites had been identified where nineteenth-century bindery records were stored. Of course, there was no guarantee *The Silver King* was at either of them. And we'd have to wait until Monday to find out—neither of the warehouse companies kept weekend hours.

Mike was smart, you had to give him that. Last night

when Vince and I had started to report our progress, we learned he'd been keeping track of the two Japanese. He knew before we told him that they had been arrested at Fountaingrove.

"Biff Okada and Slim Takehara, big bad Jap detectives," Mike had scoffed. "Some threat *they* are. Strong of breath and weak of brain."

Frannie had given him a reproving glance, and sweetly suggested that she wanted to hear what Vince and I had to report.

By the time Vince and I had finished our story about Birdie, or rather Myrna, Mike had changed his tune. "We got to get hold of her," he said. "Maybe they already have the woman. They could be pumping her for information—no telling what the hell they'll do; those guys are playing hard-ball."

Mike had phoned Myrna's number repeatedly. He finally got one of her housemates, who reported that Myrna was out, she didn't know where. "Damn well didn't care, either," Mike muttered. Then he'd recruited Vince to spend today with him in an all-out attempt to track down Myrna.

Frannie was chattering happily away about the various leads we had still to follow. "You know," she said, "I just thought of one more person to talk to."

"Who's that?"

"Julie Wulff."

Morrie's wife. Of course. "Good thinking, Frannie."

"That certainly was a strange bunch of rigmarole about the raffle tickets," she continued. "I can't wait to talk to Mrs. Simoni and find out what in the world is going on."

I said nothing. Considering the deserted aspect of that house I'd seen yesterday, I wasn't very optimistic about finding Theresa Simoni at home. And, when we pulled up out front, the place looked as forlorn as ever: scraggly lawn, peeling paint, the twin cypresses encroaching on the front porch.

"Oh, dear!" Frannie remarked the minute she saw it.

We spent a few minutes on the front porch, ringing the doorbell at appropriate intervals and listening each time to the chime and the silence that followed.

I didn't want to give up, to add Adrianna's mysterious mother to the list of persons apparently missing. "Let's try the neighbors," I said. There was no answer at the house on the right, nor at the one on the left. But, across the street, I noticed an old man who had come outside to tend his vegetable garden. He unrolled a garden hose attached to a spigot at the front of the house and began applying water to his front-yard vegetable garden. But I could see that his tomatoes and zucchini vines had already been watered, as had the row of onions that bordered the sidewalk.

I nudged Frannie. "There's our informant."

We headed across the street.

He was a wizened fellow with a gnarly face, his mouth clamped on the stub of a cigar. As we approached, he took the cigar out and used it to gesture toward the Simoni house. "You looking for her?"

"Yes," Frannie said. "Do you know if Mrs. Simoni is at home?"

"Hah! Some days it don't make no difference."

I wondered what he meant. "We wanted to talk to her," I said.

He tossed down the hose and took his time turning off the water at the spigot. "You wanna talk to her,"—he inclined his head to indicate the house across the street—"you gotta come early in the day." He made a gesture, holding his hand with the thumb and little finger out, and made a tilting movement toward his mouth.

A drinking problem. I might have guessed.

"When she's going at it . . ." He shrugged. "Maybe she's home, maybe she's not. No difference."

I remembered what Mrs. Voss had said. Or rather her neighbor. Something about Theresa having decided to straighten up and fly right. "Are there times when she isn't drinking?" I asked.

"Yah. Before breakfast—sometimes." The words were harsh but his face reflected more sadness than disapproval. "The last few days, all the time."

"I'm so sorry to hear that," Frannie said, sounding altogether distressed.

"Do you know her daughter?" I asked.

He shrugged, looking carefully off into the distance. This was a small town. He almost certainly knew exactly who she was, where she lived.

"The artist lady? I seen her go in the house. She's the one sends her to that dry-out place sometimes."

"But do you *know* the daughter, do you know Adrianna Knaupp?"

"I don't go sticking my nose in."

"How do you know she's been drinking?" I persisted. "Have you seen her?"

"When she's drinking you don't see her—that's how you know. A damn shame, and her just back from the dry-out place again, too. Couple of times she went there, she didn't drink afterwards for quite a while. This time . . ." He shrugged, then made the drinking gesture again. "Right away."

"Gracious!" Frannie said, sounding aghast. "Perhaps something happened to cause her to . . . you know."

"Nah. She just drinks. Well, sometimes it's a man sets her off." He turned and spat expertly in the direction of his onion plants. "I don't know what kind of man wants to get a woman that way, giving her liquor."

"A man came to see her?"

"Yah. He thought he was slick, parked his car down the street. I saw him."

"What did he look like?"

"Looked too good to be doing what he did. Nice clothes. Nice car—big one, same kind like yours, only older."

We were driving Frannie's Mercedes.

"A Mercedes?"

He looked uncomfortable, unwilling to say more. "Maybe so."

This could be the "nice man" Mrs. Voss had thought was one of Adrianna's clients. "Did he have light-colored hair?"

He didn't answer at first but turned his back to us, moved to the side of the house, and began unfastening the hose from the spigot.

Interview concluded, I thought. But then he spoke. "You see the daughter, you tell her she better come get her mama again." He coiled the hose expertly, and then surprised me by answering my question. "Yah. He had yellow hair." He shifted the coiled hose to his shoulder. "Damn shame," he added, as much to himself as to us, and disappeared around the side of the house.

"Oh, dear," Frannie said. "It does sound like it was the same man who came to see Adrianna."

I turned to look again at the neglected house across the street. The garbage can was still on its side near the curb.

"Nothing more we can do here," I said.

But before we left I went back across the street, picked up the garbage can, and set it right side up at the corner of the lawn.

$\triangledown$

14

"IT WAS A DAMN parade, trying to follow Myrna Purcell," Mike grumped. "The woman driving around in that cruddy Volkswagen of hers, the Japs following her, and Vince and me following them." He banged the palm of his hand on the table. Frannie flinched.

We had assembled in Frannie's kitchen, her hospitality having evolved from Chocolate Delights and patio-room formality to almond toffee ice cream in her breakfast nook. Mike's Obnoxious Quotient, it seemed to me, had become far worse with his fixation on finding *The Silver King*.

"It wasn't easy, neither, staying out of sight," Vince added. "Especially when she went to that fancy place where Morrie Wulff lives."

Ms. Floppy Hat and Morrie Wulff. An interesting development.

Vince had already finished his ice cream. Frannie asked if he wanted more. He nodded yes.

"Jeez! We had to watch out for her seeing us, *and* the Japs." He struggled to pull a handkerchief out of his back pocket, then wiped his moist brow. October days are usually warm in Sacramento. Today had been quite warm.

"Yeah," Mike said. "Morrie's place is something else. Movie-time stuff—double row of big magnolia trees going down a long driveway, wrought-iron gate with electronic security, a mansion loaded with turrets and arches."

"Right," Vince added, starting in on his second bowl of ice cream. "It was real fancy, but sure tough for surveillance. No cover, just flat ground, not even any low branches on the trees."

"Let me get this straight," I said. "You picked up Myrna's trail when she left her house. And the two Japanese, Okada and Takehara, were also following her. And she went to the Wulff place."

"Silverado Museum first," Vince said.

The museum visit wasn't surprising. "She stay at the museum long?"

Vince pulled out his notebook. "An hour and forty minutes."

"And then she went to Morrie's?"

Vince again consulted his notebook. "Fifteen minutes there."

"All of it spent trying to get in." Mike said. "She used the phone at the gate first. Then it looked like she was trying to jigger the gate control with something—credit card, probably."

"I can't imagine why she'd be trying to get in at Morrie Wulff's place," Frannie said.

"That's easy," Vince said. "She's the one found the evidence about the Stevenson book, right? And Morrie Wulff has a lot of money, and she knows he's into the Stevenson thing. Maybe she's trying to sell him information."

Mike cast a surprised look at Vince. "You could be right."

"Vince!" Frannie exclaimed. "That's wonderful thinking."

"Yeah," Mike grumbled. "If the Japs figure *that* out . . ."

"Where did she go next?" I asked.

"To this place in Calistoga," Vince said. "The New Spain Spa."

"Why would she go there?" I wondered aloud.

"The place has the best masseur in the valley," Mike reminded us. "Maybe the little lady wanted a massage."

Vince looked at him, perplexed. "Aw, that couldn't be right. She don't have that kind of money."

Mike smirked at me. I ignored him, concentrating on the puzzle of why Myrna had gone to New Spain.

"So what happened next?" Frannie prompted Mike.

"She went inside. We stayed outside. Then nothing, until our Jap buddies decided to leave."

"Which meant you had a decision to make," I said.

"Yeah." Mike was glum. "I figured old Myrna was going to stay put for a while and I wanted to know what the Japs were up to. So we followed them."

"Jeez! They drove to Napa, to this motel they were staying at. They parked their car there. Then what do they do? They walk across the street to a restaurant. We high-tailed it back to the New Spain Spa—"

"—And found Myrna had gone," I supplied.

"Shit, yes."

"There's always another day," Frannie said brightly, ignoring Mike's profanity. "Maybe tomorrow will be better."

No one said anything for a few moments, as we occupied ourselves with our own thoughts.

"Say," Mike finally said, "did you know about the Manny and Morrie feud?"

It was Mike's nature to abhor a conversational vacuum.

"Those two been doing this so-called just-kidding bit since they were teenagers. You know, you read about that kind of stuff in the newspapers—a guy sends his brother, or his buddy, a birthday gift of a big load of cement that's dumped in his driveway. The other guy retaliates with outlandish stuff ordered out of catalogs. They go back and forth, every year."

"Were the Wulff twins doing that?" I asked.

"You bet your sweet bippy."

Mike had apparently researched the Wulff family thoroughly. I wondered where he got his information. Vivian? Possibly through the connections he'd made in his public relations work for Napa Sake Gardens. Not surprisingly, he soon began to regale us with the story of the Jell-O caper.

"The stunt caused a family fracas. Old man Wulff, the grandfather, the one who rounded up the family fortune, sided with Manny. Mrs. Wulff, the twins' mother, was properly horrified. By her lights, Manny had ruined the family's social standing. Morrie seemed to think the same way."

That matched what I knew, although I'd had no idea about what the Wulff grandfather had thought. Of course, I wasn't around Napa for long after that. When I finished high school, I moved away.

"Rumor has it that Morrie's sensitive to this day about what people think," Mike went on, "and that he never forgave Manny for that Jell-O stunt."

Morrie and his mother were a pair of prigs, I thought. Anyone with a normal sense of humor would have had a good laugh, poured boiling water in the toilets, and proceeded to enjoy the party.

Mike continued. "The ha-ha birthday stuff has gotten a lot more vindictive lately, at least on Morrie's side. You oughta hear what I picked up about their last birthday." Mike leaned back, lacing his hands behind his head. "First, what Manny did."

Mike was enjoying his audience hugely.

"Manny basically stuck to the funny but harmless stuff. Out at Morrie's chateau, there's this quarter-mile driveway, lined with magnolias. What Manny did, he hired a crew to go out there at night and T.P. the trees. Every damn one of them."

Frannie giggled. Vince chortled. I thought it must have been a wonderful sight—I wished I'd seen it.

"But no harm done," Vince said. "I mean, Morrie can just hire his own crew to take the stuff down. Money don't mean nothing to him."

"Right," Mike said.

Morrie's priggish sense of dignity must have been ruffled, I thought.

"Now," Mike said. "Here's the rest of the story. Get this, what Morrie did to Manny."

"Gracious . . . what?"

Mike leaned forward, propping his elbows on the table. "Okay, listen to this. One of the things that's important to Morrie is that he's always taken real good care of his body, stayed slender. It was the only way he ever scored points over his brother."

I thought of the sketch. Manny had a classic mudslide physique.

"This is background. You gotta have it to understand," Mike went on. "Aside from the stay-slender bit, Morrie has spent a lifetime trying to keep up with his brother. It's a pattern. Manny does whatever he's currently interested in, and Morrie tries to follow—but he's always behind, always busting a gut trying to play catch-up. Every time, just when he's close, Manny is off in some new direction."

"That fits in with what we learned about Manny and Morrie and the Stevenson business," I said.

"Gracious! Manny must have discovered something about *The Silver King* first. Oh, my! Morrie was trying to keep up with him."

"Yeah. Frannie, you're not letting me finish my story."

"So what did Morrie do for a birthday prank?" I prompted.

Mike again leaned back and laced his hands behind his head. "Like I said, the staying-trim business was real important to Morrie, the only thing he could do better than Manny. So he had his brother committed to a fat farm for a week."

"Oh, no!" Frannie said.

It sounded unlikely to me. "How could he do that?"

"Well, according to local gossip, Morrie's an expert on fat farms; he's been to a bunch of them. So he picks one he's never been to. They don't know him, and he goes there with padding under his clothes so he'll look heavier."

At first the idea didn't wash with me; his appearance would seem artificial. But the Wulff twins had to be close to seventy by now. One of the sad facts of getting older is that, increasingly, you can be skinny in the face and fat in the body.

"So, at the fat farm, Morrie tells them he's Manny. And he says he's gonna show up at noon on a certain day." Mike's eyes flickered from one to another of us; he was enjoying this. "He tells them no matter how much he hollers, they gotta keep him there. Then he invites Manny to meet him for lunch at the place, but on that day he stays the hell away. The fat-farm attendants recognize their man—they think—and keep Manny there."

None of us said anything at first.

"Manny let his brother get away with this?" I finally asked.

"That's the story."

It bothered Vince, too. "He didn't try to do nothing, just stayed there for a week?"

"Nothing," Mike said. "Nada. Zilch. Apparently he shrugged it off, even laughed about it afterward, according to what I heard."

We were again silent.

Frannie, taking advantage of the opportunity, got up and fetched her notepad. She'd had it ready and waiting all this time, on the kitchen counter.

"Okay, sweetheart," Mike said. "What you got?"

Sweetheart, not *sweetcakes.* Score a round for Frannie.

"We haven't had a chance yet to tell you what we learned in Clarksburg."

After the story had been told, Mike let out one of his long, low whistles. "This blond guy is starting to sound important," he said. "How can we get a lead on him?"

Vince consulted his notebook. "Adrianna Knaupp's coming back in a couple of days. She talked to him."

"Anybody got any other ideas?" Mike asked.

I had been thinking about Myrna and why she might have gone to the New Spain Spa. "If Myrna has something she's trying to sell to Morrie, she was probably trying to find him at the spa."

Mike pounced on the idea. "Right. Good possibility. We don't know whether he was there or not, but if he wasn't, she's gonna be out looking for him again today."

Where does one look for a millionaire on a Sunday? I wondered.

"I'm gonna be on Myrna's tail first thing in the morning," Mike said. "Vince, you can go to that motel in Napa and track the two Japs."

Vince moved restlessly. "No." I recognized the stubborn tone. Vince Valenti, aka Bulldog Drummond.

"What?" Mike was startled. "What's more important than tailing Myrna?"

Vince ducked his head. "I got stuff of my own to do."

$\triangledown$

15

ON SUNDAY MORNING I drove back to Oakland to meet with the McAdoos. I'd hoped to keep our session short but was frustrated at every turn.

Mrs. McAdoo was still trying to turn the place into a California craftsman, suggesting at every turn details that didn't belong there. Stained glass, for one. And she couldn't believe the front door was original stuff. I had to get my sketches from *Rehab Right* out of the truck's glove compartment before she'd defer to my expertise—upon which they'd both earlier heaped such lavish praise.

The McAdoos had been told their place would come out of escrow the first of the week—which they construed to mean the next day, Monday. Mr. McAdoo had agreed as part of the contract to pay for a two-night motel stay, and wanted me to come down Monday evening so I'd be ready to start first thing Tuesday. I resisted, knowing the erratic ways of escrows. Also, I had my own fish to fry. Monday was the day Adrianna Knaupp was scheduled to return from her Hawaiian trip.

The McAdoos finally agreed to leave the matter of the motel open. They'd phone me as soon as the house had been turned over to them, and were much reassured when I gave them Frannie's number so they could talk to her if they couldn't get hold of me.

Then, at last, I was free to head across the Bay Bridge toward San Francisco. As I drove, I munched on the cheese sandwich I'd brought with me and considered the ramifications of what I'd learned yesterday about the Wulff family. What with Manny having turned up missing and Morrie's recently displayed vindictiveness, a good case could be made for Morrie having taken some kind of wicked shortcut to getting the Stevenson book for himself. Assuming, of course, that Manny indeed had turned up a significant lead to the whereabouts of *The Silver King*.

By the time I'd crossed the bridge and taken the off ramp for San Francisco's downtown district, now mercifully abandoned by the weekday crowds, I'd almost convinced myself that the Morrie-did-something-to-Manny theory might have merit. But it did little to explain Myrna's murky behavior, Adrianna's arranged departure for Hawaii, or her mother's whereabouts, to say nothing of the mystery of the blond man.

Or the operetta hippie.

I had several times come close to persuading myself that the episode at the Valley Savings art show was a coincidence, an aberration, something that bore no relation to the puzzle I was trying to solve. Yet the man had been so palpably angry. His anger, in fact, overrode everything I remembered about him. Every expression of it was still vivid in my mind—the fierce sound of his breathing, his tensely held muscles, those tightly clenched fists. And the chilling disregard with which he had shoved aside that frail woman in the jogging suit. Something about the sketch had engendered in him a terrible rage. But what?

I was fortunate, I realized, that The Argonaut was open on a Sunday. It was located near the Union Square shopping district, which, like the tourist areas of Ghirardelli Square and Fisherman's Wharf and unlike the deserted downtown financial district, was a seven-day-a-week operation.

It took some doing to locate the person I wanted at The Argonaut; I'd had to invoke Phyllis Butterfield's name and exaggerate my connections with Holmes Book Company. But finally I talked with someone who remembered a man who wanted Stevenson-related stuff before the search for the lost manuscript became a national craze.

"We were all impressed when we got to talking about it afterwards," the slight, bespectacled clerk told me. "It was such an amazing thing that he knew in advance. Luckily, the hoi polloi don't come in here. Since the discovery was announced we've had trouble enough with the collectors who know what they're doing."

"Had a bunch of them in here, have you?"

"Starting the minute the story broke. Actually, it's been marvelous for business."

"I'm sure it has."

We stood there for a moment in chummy silence, leaning side by side on the counter by the cash register.

"You know, the Wulff fellow was phenomenal, knowing ahead of time exactly what to look for—and I mean *exactly.*"

"What did he ask for?" I asked eagerly.

"It's remarkable. Although he engaged me in conversation about Stevenson, he didn't ask for anything directly related to the author. Instead, he was interested in materials that might have to do with the Fountaingrove Colony in Santa Rosa. More than that, he wanted anything specific to the year 1880."

Bingo! "And did you have anything like that?"

"As a matter of fact, we did."

I waited, not daring to ask what had happened next.

"You said, Mrs. Chizzit, you were . . . a collector?"

"Of sorts. I have a contracting business. Collectibles are something of a sideline."

I was grateful for the convention among dealers that it's bad form to inquire too closely of another's qualifications or intentions.

"I'm sure you can admire our good fortune," the clerk

said, "in having on hand some materials that seemed to be exactly what he wanted. They were from a Santa Rosa family with a long-ago maiden aunt who, it seems, had not only resided at Fountaingrove but had been there during the period in question. There was a diary, some letters, several scrapbooks, miscellaneous programs from events at the colony."

"And did he buy it?"

"He did indeed; he was quite eager to do so."

The clerk bestowed on me a beatific smile. Manny Wulff, I presumed, had paid dearly for the maiden aunt's memorabilia.

"I remember the occasion quite vividly," the clerk went on. "There were also some photographs. It was a very impressive aggregation. And quite an armload; I carried it down to Mr. Wulff's car for him."

"And that, I suppose, is the last of it as far as you're concerned."

"Indeed." He paused. "You seem both interested and knowledgeable. I will tell you in confidence that there's one aspect of this I've puzzled over ever since."

"What was that?"

"Mr. Wulff's attitude. Not only did he have this remarkable information—that he should look for items related to Fountaingrove—but his interest was intense. However, once he'd discovered we had the materials, he suddenly lost interest. When we went over the inventory for the collection, he scarcely listened."

Odd. "But he bought them."

"Yes. Absolutely. As I said, I went with him, outside, to help load them in his car. He opened the trunk for me and then just went around to get in the car—not so much as a backward glance to make sure the materials were properly put in his trunk. He looked back at me once, after I'd closed the trunk lid, but only to wave good-bye."

"That does sound strange."

"It is, absolutely. When collectors make a find, they don't

ignore it after the purchase. They watch closely what happens to the materials. But this Wulff person, as I said, lost
interest even before he paid for his purchase. And certainly
long before I loaded it into his trunk."

The ways of the very rich, I thought, I never would understand.

$\triangledown$

16

"THERESA SIMONI IS DEAD."

Vince dropped this bombshell on us Sunday night, when we'd again congregated at Frannie's. We sat in stunned silence for a moment.

Frannie murmured, "Oh, dear."

"Christ on a crutch," Mike said softly. Then, in his more usual tone of voice, he challenged Vince. "How do you know?"

"I went over to Clarksburg yesterday." He paused, rubbing his nose. "The reason I went, I wanted to make sure Adrianna Knaupp was okay. I checked her house."

So that's why he'd refused to say what he wanted to do; he'd had breaking and entering in mind.

"But there wasn't nothing wrong there. And the place looked like she'd gone on a vacation—a suitcase-size empty spot on the top shelf in the closet, empty hangers."

Mike stirred restlessly. "So?"

"So next I looked for Theresa Simoni." Vince ran a hand through his sparse hair. "It turns out no one in the neighborhood had seen her since last Wednesday. Five days— that's not good. I decided I better go down to the Yolo County sheriff's office and file a missing person's report. Come to find out, they fished a body out of the river Friday night. Looks like it's her."

I closed my eyes, seeing again that forlorn house, the dusty cypresses by the porch, the garbage can on its side by the curb. But I'd feared that Theresa Simoni was inside, drinking and oblivious—not that she might be dead.

Mike leaned forward, all business. "Was there an autopsy?"

"Cases like this, they got to have one. No official autopsy report yet, but the unofficial skinny is that she'd been drinking. Also, she had a lump on the back of her head."

"Do you remember what we learned from the neighbor across the street?" Frannie asked me.

"There was a man who came to see her, apparently the same blond man who'd come to Adrianna's. He parked his car down the street."

Frannie nodded somberly.

Mike straightened, sitting away from the table and impatiently placed his hand palm down on the table's surface. "The way I see it," he said, "we've got two possible scenarios here."

My hackles rose. Even at a time like this he was jockeying for position, posturing to let us know he was in charge here.

"Scenario number one," Mike said. "It's not very sexy, but we got to consider it. Theresa Simoni is wandering by the river, three sheets to the wind. She falls down, bumps her head, and tumbles into the water."

"Your scenario doesn't work," I told him. "You haven't thought it through. Think—she's walking by the river's edge, unsteady on her feet, and she stumbles." I paused, trying to rein in my anger. "She's tripped over a tree root or an uneven place in the path. Visualize what happens next, Mike."

"Okay. She stumbles, pitches forward." He was silent for a moment. "Which doesn't get her a lump on the back of the head," he conceded.

I went on, determined to skewer him. "Suppose she falls backward, something happens so that she falls backward."

"She hits the back of her head," Mike supplied. "On a rock, maybe."

"And then what happens?"

Mike was again momentarily silent. "She's down for the count. She stays where she is."

"I know what happened," Frannie said, her brown eyes luminous with sorrow. "The blond man killed her. He came to see her, gave her liquor, and then he killed her."

$\triangledown$

17

Wᴵᴛʜ Tᴇʀᴇsᴇᴀ Sɪᴍᴏɴɪ ᴅᴇᴀᴅ, I was more worried than ever about Manny Wulff's safety.

I'd spent a restless night and had awakened Monday morning trying to pull together the elements of a dimly remembered dream, the last image of which had been the sketch from the bank art show—Manny, in his turned-back-to-look-at-you pose, with the same infectious, who-cares grin. No. His expression in the dream image had been more serious; he seemed to beckon to me.

A minute later, fully awake, I decided I needed my head examined.

Nonetheless, I begged off from accompanying Vince in his rounds that morning and went on a mission of my own. My plan: Check out all the messenger services in the Napa area and see if I could find the one that had been called to pick up the sketch at Valley Savings. There couldn't be too many, not in a town the size of Napa. And whoever had picked up Manny's sketch, the assignment wasn't the sort that would be easily forgotten—it's not your everyday work, fetching the nude picture of a local millionaire from a bank his family owns.

I stopped at a gas station at the south edge of Napa, and

checked Messenger Services in the local yellow pages. Several out-of-town courier outfits were listed, but the rest were local cab companies. I decided to check the locals first, and started with the top one on the list.

The answer came right after the first ring, although the connection crackled with static. "Thank you for calling A-Cab." The voice, male, had an odd lilt to it—he'd emphasized *A-Cab.*

"Do you have a messenger service?" I asked.

"Yes, indeedy. Any size chore, door to door. What's your pleasure, ma'am?"

Good grief! "I'd like to talk to you."

"Talk away. I'm cruising. Haven't got a fare, haven't got a care."

Under any other circumstances I would have thought this great fun. "Have you got someplace you can talk to me in person?" I asked. "An office?"

"Not exactly an office, but I got a place to perch in my brother-in-law's shop. You know P and J Automotive on South Coombs Street?"

I said I'd find it. "My name's Emma," I added. "Who do I ask for?"

"Just ask for A-Cab." He chuckled. "See how the name works?"

P and J Automotive was a grubby repair shop. A battered taxi with an oversize whip antenna pulled up just as I arrived. From it, a young man of Ichabod Crane proportions extricated himself. He waved at me, then turned around to pull off his cap and sling it onto the front seat of the cab. He had a head of wildly frizzy brown hair and bulging blue eyes that gave his face a comic appearance. "Anybody call A-Cab?"

I walked over. "I'm Emma. Emma Chizzit."

When I'd said my last name he reacted with exaggerated surprise, doing a pretend double take. "Lookee here, mates," he said in a fake Australian accent. "It's Mrs. How-much-is-it."

"You're on to me," I said, and stuck out my hand. "The last name's my private joke. But the first name's always been Emma."

"I'm Bizz Wilkens. Bizz to my friends. Lawyers and strangers can call me Homer. What do you need?"

"There's a job you might have done about a week ago. I'm trying to locate the messenger service that took an assignment to pick up the sketch of a nude man from a bank art show."

"You found your man."

It took a minute to sink in. This was too easy.

He grinned. "I'm first on the list in the yellow pages." He added a wink to the grin. "I get lots of customers that way. Otherwise, I listen in on the radio chatter of the other outfits. Anybody calls a cab from a spot I can get to first, I'm in luck. I just stick my head in the door and ask if anybody called *a cab*." He favored me with another wink. "It's legal, you know—sort of."

I supposed he had to make a living any way he could, not that I thought his tactics were quite ethical. But nonetheless I was glad to have been spared the task of questioning a long list of messengers and cabdrivers. "Do you keep records of your pickups and deliveries?"

"Sure. But nobody's gonna forget this picture." He waggled his eyebrows and made his eyes boggle. Then he reached into his cab to bring out a log book. "I got a name and credit card number right here for the guy that ordered it."

This puzzled me. The people at the bank said the artist had called to withdraw the picture. "A man ordered it?"

"All I know is what I got here. The pickup was ordered by Morrie Wulff. I recognized the name right off."

"You're sure?"

"Lady, would I make this stuff up?"

It made sense, I realized, given what I knew about Morrie Wulff. He'd get the picture out of the family bank ASAP.

"Where did he want the picture delivered?"

"Nowhere. He said to hang on to it, he'd come pick it up. Only he hasn't, not yet."

"You've still got the picture?"

"Hanging just inside; we view it with great pride."

I acknowledged his humor with a shake of my head. "Can I see it?"

"Be my guest."

I followed him inside the shop to a tiny, grubby office. There on the wall was Manny Wulff in all his slab-sided glory—hand on hip, coquettish grin, everything.

"The people at the bank gave it to you just like this?" I asked. I was astonished that it wouldn't have been wrapped and put safely under cover.

"Nah. They had it all wrapped up." He grinned and favored me with another wink. "Just like nobody in Napa would know what it was if they put it in a plain brown wrapper."

"But you knew."

"Sure as hell did."

"And you took the wrappings off?"

"Why not? I thought the office could use a little high-class art."

I took my time studying the picture. I'd remembered it so many times that I'd begun to wonder how much was memory and how much was imagination. But my recollection was entirely accurate. There was that same direct gaze, the same devil-may-care, *je ne sais* what-the-hell *quoi* grin. Wherever he was, I hoped he was safe.

I thanked Bizz Wilkens for his trouble, then hurried back to Sacramento.

I pulled into our driveway long before noon, but Vince had arrived before me. His dusty Chevy was already parked in the porte cochere, and he hurried out to greet me. He'd been waiting a half-hour, impatient and eager to be off to Clarksburg. By Vince's expectations the two of us should have spent all day staking out Adrianna's house.

"She's catching a flight from Hawaii; there's a time difference," I'd told him when we were making our plans. "It'll be afternoon at least before she's home, probably late in the day."

"I don't want to take a chance on missing her. I told you.

I bet by now she's got a notice on her door to call the Yolo County Sheriff's people—well, they could have been by. I made the I.D. on her yesterday, they might have started a man on the case. Besides, how do we know when she's gonna show up? Maybe those were bargain-basement tickets; she could be coming over on a red-eye flight."

Bulldog Valenti had spoken.

"I'll be back before noon, Vince," I had reassured him. And I was, but it was scarcely early enough to suit him.

We arrived in Clarksburg far too early, of course; as I'd expected, I'd let myself in for a tedious wait.

"Didn't Adrianna's landlady say her neighbor had taken her to the airport?" I asked.

Vince grunted. "Yeah. She did say something."

"I would imagine she'll pick up Adrianna, too.

Vince took out his pocket notebook and flipped through the pages. "The neighbor is a Mrs. Wilson, lives on the corner in a two-story brown house."

The house was right up the street, in plain sight. A woman was hanging clothes on a clothesline in the side yard; a battered white Volkswagen van was parked in the driveway.

"It seems to me," I said, "that there won't be much doing until we see Mrs. Wilson leave."

Vince merely grunted. Bulldog on the job. I knew he wouldn't be persuaded to leave; we settled into another long silence.

"I wonder how Mike and Frannie are doing, checking out those bindery sites," I said at last.

Vince shrugged. He wasn't much interested in finding the lost manuscript, and hadn't been all along. As far as he was concerned, this was a case of a missing person and now, a murder.

We'd agreed yesterday that trying to talk to Adrianna before she learned of her mother's death was the right thing to do. The approach seemed ghoulish but, I reassured myself, talking to her now would be far kinder than disturbing her in her grief.

Finally, sometime after four o'clock, we saw Mrs. Wilson

emerge from the house and get into the old van. Much later, the van reappeared and Mrs. Wilson dropped Adrianna off in front of her house.

Vince was out of the car like a shot. I trailed behind as he hurried to the porch.

"Ms. Knaupp?" he queried. She'd just been reaching for a business card wedged between her screen door and the door frame. She turned, giving us her attention.

"Yes." She looked at Vince inquiringly. I hoped she thought the card was about something routine, maybe something a salesperson had left.

"Vince Valenti," he said. "Fairville Police."

Looking surprised, she set down her suitcase.

"The lady and I have a few questions to ask you."

"I'm Emma Chizzit," I said, offering no explanation.

Adrianna was a slender young woman—a dishwater blond who wore little makeup but had a certain attractiveness. An *artless* look, I thought, one she probably invested a great deal of care in creating.

"What do you want?" she asked, glancing at each of us in turn.

"Ma'am, we need to know what visitors you might have had right before you went away on your trip."

"Is something wrong?"

"We just got to have the answers to a few questions," Vince said. He took out his notebook. "Now, you won this trip in a raffle. We want to know about the man who sold you the tickets."

"Wasn't he on the up-and-up?" she asked anxiously.

Vince didn't answer her. He was doing *cop.* Superbly. I never cease to be astonished at the way people will take for granted his right to ask questions.

"He *was* kind of strange," Adrianna said. "I mean, he was wearing an obvious toupée. But he was sweet, a real amateur about selling the tickets. He fumbled with the change and all. He seemed so nice, and he said his church needed the money. I had no idea there might be a problem.

Was there something wrong with taking the tickets?"

"We just want to confirm he came to see you, ma'am."

"Oh."

"Now, there was someone else, someone who came to see you before this man did."

"Yes. Another man. He wanted me to . . . sketch him. He'd phoned for an appointment before he came. We talked for a while, and then he said he wanted to think it over." She shrugged.

I closed my eyes. This visitor had been the blond man. "What did he look like?" I asked.

"He was about forty, but in very good shape. Muscular. Nice bone structure to his face. Scandinavian, I'd say; he was quite blond."

"Ma'am, it's important we know everything we can about this man."

"He had very good manners, drove a nice car—an older Mercedes. But . . ."

She hesitated, as when she'd said he wanted her to sketch him. "Was there something unusual about the work he wanted you to do?" I asked.

"A nude sketch. Not all *that* unusual. And I've got a policy; I always have a third person present for the sitting." She sighed. "In my business you have to know how to deal with the nudie-pose creeps."

Vince grunted. "You think he was one of those?"

She tipped her head to one side, obviously considering her answer. "Not exactly. But it was odd; he wanted a very specific pose."

"What was that, ma'am?"

"He demonstrated—stood there with his back to me, looking over one shoulder. Kind of a funny pose for a man."

"But it was the same pose you did for the picture in the art show!" I blurted.

She looked at me blankly.

"Did he say what he would be doing with the picture?" I asked, ignoring her confusion.

"No."

"Can you tell us his name?" I was unable to conceal my eagerness.

She studied me. "No." She paused, her thoughts apparently again returning to the blond man. "Come to think of it, he never introduced himself."

"Did you make a sketch of him?" Vince asked.

"No." She was becoming more and more uneasy. Her gaze wandered to the white card on her door.

"Ma'am, a sketch that looked just like the pose you described was entered in an art show."

She looked at Vince, registering mild confusion.

"The sketch was of a man named Manny Wulff. Do you know him?"

"No." She looked more perplexed than ever.

"Your name was signed to the sketch."

She looked blank for another moment, then her expression changed to something between sadness and resignation. She sighed heavily. "It might have been one of my mother's . . . misadventures." She was embarrassed and disconcerted, for the moment forgetting to be dubious about us, forgetting the card on the door.

The sketch had not been made by Adrianna but by her mother. And I was certain Frannie was right—the blond man, whoever he was, had killed Theresa Simoni.

"Thank you very much for your help," I said to Adrianna.

I grabbed Vince by the arm. We left hurriedly. The card on her door had to be from someone at the sheriff's department. I desperately hoped we'd be out of sight before she looked at it.

$\triangledown$

18

WHEN VINCE AND I got back from Clarksburg I learned
that the McAdoos had phoned. Four times. Their house was
out of escrow. Could I come down that night after all? Surely,
I would show up tomorrow morning—could I be there by 8
A.M.? And was I *truly* certain they shouldn't have a front
door that was a bit more rustic?

Duty called, to say nothing of financial need.

I phoned the McAdoos. My annoyance increased when I
heard the click of their answering machine taking over the
line, and then Mrs. McAdoo's all-too-pert recorded message.
I imagined them out to dinner at some trendy place—whatever
was the restaurant of the week for Oakland's stylish
couples—and then my annoyance overcame my common
sense. I left a curt message. All I could promise, I said, was
that I would be down before the end of the week.

After I'd hung up, I felt a brief pang of guilt for leaving the
McAdoos up in the air—but only the briefest of pangs. After
all, I told myself, I couldn't imagine a worse time to have to
drop everything and go down to the job in Oakland. Mike,
obsessed with beating out his Japanese rivals in the search
for *The Silver King*, had taken over Frannie completely. The
two of them had spent all day in south San Francisco, fruit-

lessly searching old bindery files; they were going back to-morrow and would stay with it until they found some trace of the Stevenson galleys. Vince, with his bulldog determina-tion to find the man who'd murdered Theresa Simoni, had given top priority to talking again to the sheriff's deputies in Yolo County. "That blond man could have a record there," he declared. "I bet he's got a record more places than one, rap sheets as long as your arm."

I loaded my truck early Tuesday morning with the tools and equipment I needed for the McAdoo job; I'd decided after all to start as promised. Still, my mind was on leads I wanted to pursue—for starters, looking up Morrie Wulff. When I'd gone over to The Argonaut on Sunday I'd intended to stop on the way back and get the addresses and phone numbers from the business cards Morrie and Manny had left at Holmes Book Company. But I had forgotten the errand.

Increasingly, I worried about Manny Wulff. But once I presented myself at the McAdoo house I'd be lost to the demands of Mr. and Mrs. M. until the job was finished. They'd not give me a moment's peace until the work was done.

"Rats!" I said aloud.

I drove west on the freeway, feeling altogether frustrated, and was halfway to Oakland before I thought of something else, something Frannie had told me about Julie Wulff. Julie was in charge of her father's estate. Frannie had particularly mentioned the house he and his second wife had in the Napa hills. The stepmother was a retired ballet dancer, or some such, and had had the house built to her specifications. "Everyone thought Julie might move out there after her fa-ther died; the second wife had long since flown the coop. But Vivian told me Julie despised the house. So, now that she and Morrie are separated, she's staying at an apartment in Napa her father also owned."

Maybe, I thought, I could find out something useful from Julie Wulff. The McAdoos could stew in their own juice, at least for an hour or two, I thought, and turned off Highway

80 and headed for Napa and the nearest phone booth. Julie had been a McDonald. There were two initials-only McDonald entries in the directory, and Kevin Douglas McDonald.

I dialed the Kevin Douglas McDonald number. Julie Wulff answered the phone.

I told her I had grown up in Napa and remembered her husband and brother-in-law—which was true, as far as it went. I told her I was trying to locate Manny—also true— and that I wanted to come see her. She agreed, no questions asked.

Julie was somewhere around thirty—not beautiful, but slender and very pretty with small, regular features and a mane of wavy brown hair. She greeted me with finishing-school poise but nonetheless looked a nervous wreck. "I'm just *so* glad you came. I feel much better, knowing I'm not the only one worried about Manny. I'm *really* worried—no one else is, you know. I guess it's selfish of me, but when he's not in town I don't have *anyone* I can talk to. And Morrie's just gotten so . . . so . . ."

As she talked she held her hands clasped together, her fingers constantly twining, her knuckles white. Classic Hysterical Female, I thought. And forgave myself.

"It was different when my father was still alive, you know. And then Mr. Wulff died, too, Morrie's father. It's so hard, having to make decisions all on my own."

I made sympathetic noises at what seemed the appropriate times and watched, fascinated, as her hands moved and the fingers writhed. "Tell me why you're worried about Manny," I asked at the first opportunity.

"Well, I can't explain it, I just *am*. I mean, that business with the picture was so *strange*. And don't you see? Nobody will take me seriously. Manny's secretary knows he didn't use those airline tickets but she just says he always does crazy things." She scarcely paused for breath. "Have you heard about those awful jokes Morrie and Manny play on each other?"

"A little, yes."

"I was taken aback when Morrie and I first got married, I mean, to learn they were doing that—they took it so *seriously* and all. And then I got to thinking it was just good fun, at least some of it. But now Morrie's gotten so . . ." She abruptly looked off into the distance.

"What I don't understand," she said after a moment, "is why Manny would do something like that—put his picture in the bank and then not be around to watch the fun."

"I don't either," I said.

"And especially since he *promised* he'd be around to help me."

"What did he promise to help you with?"

"My father's estate. It's still in probate, after all this time, and just *so* complicated."

"Surely you have lawyers who can—"

"But lawyers are—well, you know. And Manny promised to help me with the property settlement with Morrie, too."

"I understand you two are divorcing."

"Yes. And it's the strangest thing, the last time I talked to Morrie he jumped all over me about my father's estate— as if it were any business of his. For instance, he asked me which real estate agent was handling the rental of the house my father and his wife lived in. We don't need the rent money, so why should Morrie be after me like that? He kept saying I needed to do a better job of *managing the resource*."

I murmured something. Julie continued at full tilt.

"Oh, I just don't know what's going on. I'd give anything to know where Manny is."

"Do you have any ideas—possibilities where he might be?"

Julie started to cry silently. Tears spilled out of her eyes and slid down her face. I waited, letting her weep, then fetched a tissue. When she'd gotten mopped up a bit, I asked her what bothered her so much.

It was another minute before she answered. "It's Morrie," she whispered.

"You're afraid Morrie will do something to you?"

She shook her head. "He'll do something to Manny, I just know it." The tears started again. She seemed close to hysteria.

I led her to the sofa, sat her down, and comforted her into quietude. "You can tell me, Julie. Tell me what's wrong." I felt like a con artist, exploiting her misery.

It took a long time to get it all out. Julie was convinced Morrie had kidnapped Manny, and not just because of the fat-farm incident. On the Fourth of July, Morrie had hosted a barbecue—a rather out-of-character thing for him to do because he'd done no other entertaining since their separation. And he'd tried to get Manny drunk, Manny had told her later, but Manny had smelled a rat and left the party.

"It was a kidnap attempt, don't you see?"

I kept my silence; I had no idea what to make of the incident.

"I keep thinking something awful has happened." She started sobbing.

I stood up. "Let's go take a look at Manny's house." She gazed at me in surprise.

"That's as good a place as any to start if we want to find out where he is."

She agreed readily. Half an hour later we were standing on the back patio of his secluded apartment.

"Does he have an alarm system?" I asked.

"No." Julie shrugged. "He's not like Morrie—Morrie keeps everything locked up. He's got this terribly complicated alarm system, you know, and I was always setting it off by accident. Morrie would get *just* furious."

While she talked I checked the doors and windows. We were in luck—I was able to get the patio's sliding glass door off its track.

Remembering Vince's search of Adrianna's house, I suggested we look for luggage.

"Oh, he always takes his big carpetbag for carryon luggage; he had it with him every time we took him to the airport."

She made a beeline for the bedroom and a walk-in closet. "He never goes anywhere without it."

It was gone. She shook her head in confusion. "He couldn't be on vacation, I just know it."

With the array of clothing in the closet, I'd never be able to surmise whether he'd taken any of it. Julie seemed as stumped as I was. "I don't know," she said. I don't know what to do now." She looked ready to start crying again.

"Let's look at the rest of the place," I said. "Does he have a desk?" I thought we might find an appointment calendar, perhaps a scribbled note indicating plans for something other than the trip for which he'd bought airline tickets.

Julie led the way across the huge living room. The furniture was leather—large, expensive, and very comfortable-looking. The bedroom had been, surprisingly, an impersonal place, but here I caught the flavor of Manny's personality and varied interests. The room was filled with bookshelves, display cases, and odd memorabilia, the walls covered with primitive art, masks, shields, photos, and maps. In one corner stood an oversize globe of the world.

The coffee table was surprisingly bare, except for three books arranged side by side. They were obviously old editions. I took a closer look—all were by Robert Louis Stevenson.

"Look at that," Julie said, indicating the books. "He's been collecting Stevenson since last spring. That's what got to Morrie," she said, her voice rising as if she were determined not to cry.

"Do you think he's trying to beat Manny out at finding the missing manuscript?"

She started crying all over again.

I abandoned her to start checking out the apartment on my own. I opened a door off the kitchen and found myself in the garage. A battered Saab was parked there.

"Is this Manny's car?" I called to Julie.

She came out of her funk long enough to come and have a look in the garage. "Yes."

"I want to open the trunk."

She shrugged, indicating she couldn't help me. I poked around in the garage and in the kitchen looking for a spare set of keys. I found them finally, hanging on a nail just inside the door from the garage into the kitchen. I opened the trunk and found a cardboard carton, taped shut, an Argonaut label pasted on. Apparently Manny hadn't touched it.

Curiouser and curiouser.

I replaced the car keys and continued the inspection of Manny's apartment. In an alcove off the front hall was a telephone and a small desk. The desk was bare and tidy, the message light on the answering machine blinking.

I punched "Play Messages" and listened. At the same time I started going through the drawers in the desk. There seemed to be nothing of significance, nor was there anything useful in the first few telephone messages. Then, in the bottom drawer, I found a large manila envelope. I pulled it out and opened it. Inside was a small stack of papers—old stuff, frayed and discolored. The one on top bore an 1880 date and the salutation "My dearest Charles."

I heard a familiar voice on the tape.

"Mr. Wulff, this is Helen Chaffee at Silverado Museum. We're terribly anxious to know if you've heard yet from the people who were to authenticate the Stevenson documents. As you can well imagine, we're being hounded by reporters." She paused, sounding somewhat embarrassed. "Actually, I can't blame them for getting restless. Surely you can let us know when you might expect to hear."

So Manny was the anonymous donor to the museum who had volunteered to have the documents authenticated— only he'd done nothing of the sort.

Julie, still sniffling, had come over to stand beside me. "It's probably another prank. When Morrie finds out . . ."

"Maybe it's not a prank." I'd been studying the letter. "This sure looks real to me." It reeked of authenticity. The paper was brittle, the spidery script written in faded ink. Lower on the page was another handwriting, more forceful, darker, and a message about "financial salvation at last."

"The curator said there were letters started by Stevenson and finished by his wife," I told Julie. "This sure looks like one of them."

"It's a prank!" Julie shouted wildly. "But Morrie doesn't know it. He just thinks . . ." She clutched at my arm. "Oh, my God! Morrie really has taken him away, and he's . . . he's . . ." She burst into tears again.

The girl was too much. It took me awhile, but I got her hugged and patted into some semblance of composure. Then I let us out of Manny's house, after making sure we'd left no trace of our visit.

All the way back to her place I listened to her and comforted her and reassured her. Morrie hadn't discovered anything about what Manny had been doing, whatever it was, I said. And even if he had, he still probably hadn't kidnapped Manny. Surely Manny was somewhere safe, somewhere nearby; he was watching everything that was going on, and laughing.

I made it all sound completely plausible, and by the time I left her Julie was much calmed.

I hadn't believed a word I'd said.

$$\triangledown$$

19

I DIDN'T KNOW WHETHER the documents were fake or
genuine, or if Morrie really had abducted Manny. But one
thing Julie had said stuck in my mind: Morrie had asked
about the long-empty house that had belonged to her
father.

The McAdoos could wait a bit longer. I went to a pay
phone and started calling realtors, finally connecting with
the man who handled the McDonald place.

"My golly," he said. "Where'd you hear about it? I haven't
had a nibble in months."

"Just word of mouth. I was looking for . . . um . . . a place
for some friends who are coming over from Europe and plan
to stay a few months."

"Just the ticket! This house is in an estate—still fully
furnished, fully equipped, and for sale or for rent, either one.
It's a grand place; the folks who used to live there called it
Hummingbird House."

"Sounds good," I said.

"Secluded, lots of privacy. Interesting layout, by the way.
And lots of special features, nice setup for entertaining."

"Just what I had in mind," I said.

"You want to look at the place tomorrow?"

"Actually, I'd like to see it now."

But he couldn't show it to me today.

"My schedule for tomorrow is a little iffy," I told him. "Why don't you give me directions. I can do a drive-by and be back in touch."

I wrote down the instructions: Silverado Trail up the east side of the valley, Howell Mountain Road to Conn Valley Road, then five miles on Conn Valley and take the unmarked fork to the left. There was a HUMMINGBIRD HOUSE sign at the driveway, the realtor said.

I considered calling the police. But Manny wasn't officially missing. What would I tell them? I didn't want to admit breaking into his home. The sane thing to do was check out the house first; the only reason to make a report would be if someone were there.

It took me a full half-hour to drive up the east side of the valley to Howell Mountain Road. Silverado Trail, normally uncrowded on a weekday, was almost bumper to bumper, at least at the outset. Treasure seekers still crowded the Napa Valley, a tide of human lemmings. I didn't envy the folks living here—I imagined by now that people had probably put padlocks on every old outbuilding and shed. And rummaged through the contents themselves in their off hours.

Traffic had thinned by the time I neared Howell Mountain Road. The hills flanking the eastern edge of the valley rose precipitously here, taller and dryer and more barren than their counterparts across the valley to the west. The grass, desiccated by a summer's worth of heat, was more beige than golden; the roadside oaks and the occasional hillside digger pine looked dispirited and droopy. Only the manzanita seemed to flourish.

When I had been a girl, this side of the valley had been virtually uninhabited, but now I saw clusters of mailboxes at intervals along the side of the road, marking those scourges of the New West, ranchettes.

When I turned on to Conn Valley Road I noted the mileage. Precisely five miles later, I spotted the unmarked turnoff that led north. I drove slowly on the winding road, with the truck window down, taking in the quiet of the countryside and the dusty smell of the pavement. No more mailboxes here, no branching driveways. And, thank the Lord, no cutesy fences or countrified mobile homes. Silence hung in the air, unbroken except for the buzz of an occasional cicada. I almost missed the small sign.

The driveway twisted steeply uphill to my right, then disappeared out of sight in the folds of a ravine. It had been graded and graveled at one time, but several winters of rain had taken their toll; it was now hard-packed dirt, etched with little gulleys. I drove up it for almost a mile, wending my way slowly uphill. Then, after turning a sharp corner, I found myself in a wide gravel-paved turnaround area.

On the far side was a large house. The McDonald "villa," undoubtedly. It was a two-story affair, with an enclosed patio close to the front and, above that, a shallow second-story balcony. The far corner of the right wall was graced with an enormous stone chimney; I imagined the house to have a reverse floor plan, with the living room toward the back and perhaps a kitchen or dining area opening on to the enclosed patio. To the right of the house was what appeared to be a garden enclosed by a high wall; I could see the tops of plantings here and there. Even farther to the right was a three-car garage.

Hummingbird feeders were hung in the patio and on the upstairs balcony. There must have been at least ten at each level—large tubes with faded plastic orange "blossoms" at the bottoms. No hummingbirds here now; the feeders were dusty and looked disused, as did all of Hummingbird House. The shrubbery languished for lack of watering; the windows, opaque with dust, seemed to stare dully at me, reflecting a shine of late-morning sunlight.

I got out of the truck and stood staring up at the dusty, blank windows, feeling unaccountably disappointed. But someone using the house wouldn't put out a welcome mat, I realized. I looked back across the graveled area, alert for something subtle, tire tracks or footprints. But there was nothing. The area, though dusty, was clean and bare; there was no indication anyone had been here for months. I had to admit I'd been wrong; the hunch that had seemed so right had proved to be a miscue. Grateful now that I hadn't contacted the police, I got back into the truck, turned it around, and started down the long driveway.

I was nearly to the road before I realized what was wrong. The turnaround area had been too bare, too clean. I should have seen windswirls of scattered leaves and twigs, animal and bird tracks in the thick dust, an accumulation of nature's debris. The area had to have been swept to conceal tire tracks.

I was determined to have another look at the McDonald place. When I got back to the road I continued along it a quarter-mile or so until I came to a flat crest. The road widened here; it was a good place to leave my truck.

I studied the lay of the land. Uphill to my right ran the bare, flattened spine of a ridge. It would be easy to walk up there and, from the ridgetop, see across the steep ravine that ran between it and Hummingbird House.

The approach had seemed simple enough from the road, but as I got near the higher part of the ridge, I found myself farther away from the house than I'd expected—the ravine had branched. Still, even from this distance, I could see Hummingbird House. The back of the second story sported a large open balcony, a generous rooftop area bounded by a pergola—a massive trellis that would have been just right for wisteria. But nothing grew there; the pergola was bare.

My heart almost stopped. I saw movement on the balcony, a man in white clothing.

I dropped to the ground. What a fool! I'd stood in the open, in plain sight. I crawled as rapidly as I could toward the sheltering trees of the ravine between me and the house. Then I scrambled down the steep slope into it, not stopping until I was in the dry creekbed at the bottom.

I needn't have panicked, I told myself. I was much too far away. The man, busy with his own affairs, couldn't possibly have seen me. And I had to see what was going on, had to have something definite to report to the police.

The other side of the ravine, the side toward the house, was impossibly steep. I started making my way up the dry creekbed. A sizable stream must flow here in winter, I realized. The creekbed was a succession of small, dry pools with sand-and-gravel bottoms, separated by shallow, dry waterfalls. A chill of apprehension made my skin crawl as I followed the course of the stream uphill, despite the reassuring familiarity of the landscape elements.

I soon came to a large circle of gravel, the site of a pond in wetter months. Here the ravine's sides sloped upward at a more gentle angle. I moved up the slope, cautious but eager to get within view of the house, and stopped when I reached the outer perimeter of the ravine's trees. The house was just beyond an intervening grassy area, but I was too far to one side of it to see what was happening on the rooftop balcony. I edged downhill, staying near the trees.

The man in white was still on the balcony, talking in an odd manner. He gesticulated, and paced continually. I could make out only a little of what he was saying but was struck by the odd rhythm of his words. Several times he raised his voice markedly, repeating the phrase "I ask you."

I moved back until I was well under the shelter of overhanging branches, then crept a little farther downstream. After traversing what I thought would be the right distance, I again moved to the edge of the trees. "Would a reasonable man . . ." I could hear more clearly now. "I ask you, would *any* reasonable man make a choice like this?" I got down on my hands and knees and crawled forward, venturing a few feet beyond the shelter of the trees.

I could now see the balcony clearly. I was much closer than I had expected, and almost on a level with it. The pacing man fascinated me. He exuded a lithe, muscular energy— and was obviously the blond man Adrianna had described. He wore a close-fitting white T-shirt, white duck pants, white shoes.

At the far side of the balcony I saw another person, a hunched-over figure in a gray sweatshirt and pants seated in the doorway. Manny Wulff! I was certain of it. I should leave, summon the police.

I continued to watch, mesmerized by the pacing man. He continued to stride back and forth. The thought sank home: This is the man who killed Theresa Simoni.

He addressed his remarks not to Manny but apparently to some third person. This puzzled me; I could see no one. "I ask you . . ." The blond man made a sweeping gesture to indicate something in a corner of the balcony beyond my line of vision. "Here this man has delicious food. Gourmet food. Beautiful food. Is this the behavior of a reasonable man? Look at this, just look at this!"

He stooped, then stood up again with a small red-and-white checkered carton in his hand. "Pasta salad! Exquisite!" He put his fingertips to his lips and then opened them wide, blowing a kiss to the wind. "With anchovies and Greek olives. And look at this!" He brandished another container. "Ratatouille—the best! Yet he turns it down, spurns it. I ask you again, is this the behavior of a reasonable man?"

Manny ignored him, staring stolidly toward a far corner of the balcony.

The invisible third party did not exist, I concluded, except for the purposes of the blond man's oratory. And it came to me suddenly what I was witnessing was an attempt at brainwashing.

The blond man's voice dropped to a stage whisper. "I implore you . . . I beg you to understand this man," he declared to the nonexistent third person. He threw up both hands, his voice rose. "All that's needed is a few words. A few simple words." He suddenly stopped, whirled, pointed a finger at Manny. "All this time, all this trouble—any reasonable man would have given us what we wanted by now!"

Manny continued to ignore him.

The voice changed to a cajoling purr. "Any reasonable man would be enjoying this beautiful food . . . exquisite wines.

Or perhaps a hot shower . . . clean towels . . . clean clothes."
He stepped directly in front of Manny. "But *you!*" he shouted.

Manny said something I couldn't hear.

The blond man turned and directed a vehement kick in
the area where he'd set the food containers. One flew
across the patio, spraying out its contents and bouncing
against the pergola.

I'd heard and seen enough.

I moved backward on all fours, inching under the protec-
tion of the overhanging branches, trying to stay clear of the
steep drop into the ravine.

My foot slipped.

Horrified at the noise I was making, I slid and scrabbled
downward. Dry tree branches snapped; my feet scrunched
in the dry dirt as I struggled to halt my descent. And the
noise continued after I reached bottom. Not daring to move,
I listened helplessly as gravel avalanches streamed into the
creekbed around me. A crow, cawing madly, flapped up from
the treetop above me; he made a great to-do, his intruder-
in-the-forest cries continuing as he circled above the ravine.

The blond man had to have heard me.

Still crouched in fright, I held my mouth open, straining
in the sudden silence to hear even the slightest sound. And
I could still hear, faintly, the orator's cadence of the blond
man's voice. I scurried on down the little ravine and then
followed it to the larger creek along the driveway, planning
to stay out of sight until I was back at the road.

I paused only once, to take stock. The palms of my hands
were numb and scratched, and one was bleeding. Ditto for
one knee. But I'd sustained no major damage. And once I
reached the road I had only to walk the short distance to
where I'd left my truck. I hurried, staying out of sight in the
creekbed, postponing for as long as possible the need to
scramble up into the road and out into view. Then I ran up
the road toward my truck.

The blond man was there, waiting for me.

$\triangledown$

20

I spent the rest of that day—and my first night at Hummingbird House—locked in a makeshift storeroom at the rear of the garage.

I sweated in the stuffy shed all afternoon, trying to formulate plans of escape. I pushed experimentally against the door, the walls, the ceiling; I scratched with my boot sole at the hard dirt of the floor. I listened, late in the day, to the sound of the garage door opener working, my truck being pulled into the garage. With this, I squeezed back tears of disappointment—I'd been hoping against hope he'd leave the truck out on the road long enough for someone to spot it.

I was all too aware of how foolish I had been. Nobody would even realize I was in trouble. I hadn't told anyone where I was going; Frannie wasn't expecting me to come home because I'd told her the McAdoo job would probably keep me away for two nights. And, worst of all, I'd told the McAdoos I might not be on the job right away.

I thought wistfully of Vince. He knew about the McAdoo job; there was a long-shot chance he might try to get hold of me, perhaps to talk over his progress with the list of leads we'd mutually agreed needed checking. But he probably wouldn't think about checking with Julie; she wasn't on our list of leads. And he had absolutely no way of knowing about Hummingbird House.

Time dragged in my stuffy prison. Darkness came; the temperature dropped. No food was brought to me, no water. I shivered, doing my best to ignore my hunger and thirst, pinning my hopes for survival on the fact that I was still alive. I reassured myself with the idea the blond man apparently thought I might be of use to him—if not, he'd have killed me long since.

The next morning he took me upstairs, to the room adjoining the upstairs balcony in which he held Manny captive. The sliding door was open. Manny sat in the doorway much as he had yesterday. He gave me one swift, startled glance when the blond man first shoved me into the room and then, to my surprise, turned away and continued to sit and stare.

Before my captor had brought me to the room, he'd strapped my wrists with a long strip of heavy nylon fabric, knotted close to the flesh, but with a generous length of end trailing. He now attached the trailing end to a dance barre that ringed the room just inside the doorway. Manny, I noticed, was attached to the barre in the same way. The blond man took his time, working with deliberate care until he had satisfied himself that my nylon strap was attached loosely enough to allow it to slide back and forth between the barre supports, and the knots tight enough to thwart any attempt to untie them.

He then presented me to Manny.

"*Mister* Wulff, I *commend* to your attention this lady. She has most generously come to rescue you." He inclined his head to me in exaggerated mock courtesy. "Such a gallant lady, *Mister* Wulff. How lucky you must feel to have her attentions."

He studied both of us, undoubtedly searching for some clue about why I'd come. He smiled evilly at Manny. "Surely, a reasonable man such as yourself will do everything in his power to ensure the lady's safety."

He went on endlessly in his taunting orator's voice, the gist of what he said being that Manny surely would now decide to be more cooperative. He would see that the situation had changed and, being a gentleman, value my safety over mere financial reward. Who cared, really, about a dusty set of old galley proofs?

At least I now knew why he hadn't killed me.

I decided to follow Manny's example and did my best to ignore our captor's oratory. I studied the room we were in. I assumed it to be the second Mrs. McDonald's dance practice studio. The barre ran under the front windows and across one wall, the end wall of the house. It was completely covered with mirror, the glass now dusty and fly-specked. The sliding doors to the balcony made up a third wall of the room. The last, the only interior wall, had a doorway leading into a bathroom and, in a corner near the front of the house, a stairwell.

On the wall between the stairwell and the bathroom was a rack supporting a military-style automatic rifle and a peg on which hung a blackjack. Also on that wall was a telephone. A nice touch in the brainwashing scheme, I thought.

I turned my attention to the nylon leashes with which we were tethered. They were the sort of restraint, I thought, that might be used in a psychiatric facility. I judged we could move in and out the door to the balcony and slide our tethers far enough along the barre to see out the front windows. But we couldn't reach the telephone. Nor, of course, the weapons.

Our captor had stopped talking. I looked up to see him studying me.

"You will discover," he said, "that your restraints are very confining. You will be able to reach nothing on the far wall . . . nothing." He made a bow and swept an arm to indicate the things beyond reach, the telephone and the weapons. And the bathroom. A slow smile spread across his face. "Yes, *madam*, your stay here will have its . . . humiliating moments."

I glanced at Manny. He looked away.

The blond man resumed his harangue, now adding a new element: his employer.

Surely Manny could understand that the employer was becoming increasingly impatient. Surely Manny could anticipate the terrible consequences that might follow should he, our caretaker, no longer be able to protect us from the impatience of his employer.

The employer, if there was one, had to be Morrie Wulff. *Dear Lord!* Manny's own brother.

Who was the blond man? I wondered. I considered the nylon tethers, his white pants and shoes. Perhaps he'd been a psychiatric attendant—if so, he was hardly a credit to his profession. But how could Morrie Wulff have gotten involved with someone so ruthless?

The oratory went on relentlessly. The man seemed never to tire, never to run out of words. Manny stared resolutely into a far corner of the balcony, and I took advantage of the opportunity to study him.

The sketch had been a very good likeness. The squarish, pleasant face was identical—minus the grin, of course. And at the moment he didn't look much like a millionaire. He hadn't shaved recently and his hair was lank. The gray sweatsuit was baggy and stained. I turned my gaze away, not wanting to be caught staring.

I contemplated the row of high windows on the wall that faced the front of the house. Yesterday, light-years ago, I'd stared up at those windows and they'd stared blankly back at me. I remembered the patina of dust, the reflected sunlight's dull glare.

No sense thinking about it. I studied the weapons on the opposite wall, wondering where he'd gotten the attack rifle. Of the two weapons I somehow found the blackjack the more menacing. Its shank was long and slightly bent, the entire weapon sheathed in woven black leather. I had the impression of something often handled, if not often used, worn with time. Cherished. I shuddered. This was very likely the weapon used to give Theresa Simoni that bump on the back of her head.

Our captor interrupted my thoughts.

"Dear lady . . . and *Mister* Wulff." He bowed deeply, mockingly, then moved toward the stairwell. "You must now excuse me. I bid you adieu for the day."

A moment later he was gone. I started to speak, but Manny motioned me to silence. I waited, and when I thought I heard a door close downstairs, again started to speak.

"Not yet," Manny said fiercely.

We waited again. Finally, I heard the rumble of the garage door opening and after that, the unmistakable rattle of a diesel engine. I dragged my tether along the barre and peered out the front windows. Below me, I could see the blond man. He had a broom.

"He's wiping out the tire tracks," I said.

"He does it every time. Meticulous bastard."

I watched, fascinated. The Mercedes was positioned at the top of the driveway, all four wheels on the rutted hardpan, which wouldn't take much of a tire impression.

"Sometimes he doesn't really leave." Manny said. "He sneaks back up to spy."

We watched until the blond man had finished sweeping the graveled area, stowed the broom in the garage, and had gotten back into his Mercedes. The garage door rumbled shut. The car disappeared down the driveway.

"Gone for good," Manny said, "or at least for the rest of the day."

"Who is he?" I asked.

"His name is Lars Hanson." Manny flashed a grin at me, the grin so familiar from the sketch. "More to the point," he said, "who in the hell are you?"

$\triangledown$

21

I EXPLAINED TO MANNY how I'd come to be involved in this. Frannie had wanted to find *The Silver King* and we'd learned that he apparently knew about it long before others did. Then we'd seen his picture in the bank's art show and learned he was missing—after which the picture had been withdrawn and we couldn't contact the artist. I more or less glossed over the last part, reluctant to tell him Theresa Simoni was dead.

While I spoke, Manny approached a large bowl, once used for dog food, which Lars Hanson had left out on the hardwood floor. It was filled with water. Manny made a don't-pay-attention-to-this gesture, then got down on all fours and sucked thirstily at the water.

I looked away, unwilling to watch. I remembered things I'd read about brainwashing. *Harassment. Deprivation. Humiliation.* Lars Hanson knew his stuff.

Manny didn't drink very much, taking the water level down scarcely more than a half-inch. "Sorry," he said when he had finished. "I was awful goddamn thirsty." He indicated I should do as he had done. "Don't try to pick up the bowl," he advised me. "It's impossible to drink that way without spilling some."

128

He turned and looked the other way. I drank, careful to take only as much as Manny had. The experience of being down on all fours was indeed humiliating.

I continued my explanations. I finally had to tell him Theresa Simoni was dead.

"Oh, God!" Manny stood up and started pacing the short distance his tether would allow.

I studied him, wondering how to ask the circumstances under which she'd done the sketch.

"At first we thought the artist who sketched you was named Adrianna Knaupp."

"What?" he asked sharply.

"Adrianna's name was signed to the picture. She's Theresa Simoni's daughter. Theresa apparently didn't want to sign her own name." I waited, hoping he'd explain; he seemed lost in thought. "How did Theresa come to make the sketch?"

Manny sighed heavily and came to sit, cross-legged, beside me. "She sketched me when I was at Forest House. It's a treatment facility for alcoholics."

"What were you doing there?" I blurted.

"I made the excursion courtesy of our friend Lars Hanson. He knocked me out—with the blackjack that's hanging on the wall—and then filled me full of booze. I woke up there."

I didn't understand; it sounded outlandish.

"It was my brother's doing." Manny spoke slowly, choosing his words carefully. "I thought at the time it was just . . . we've spent a lifetime going back and forth with these jokes, and . . ."

"I know."

He looked at me, registering mild surprise.

"Don't forget. I had a long talk with Julie yesterday." That was a simplification of how I knew—no need telling Manny how his feud with his brother was the subject of widespread gossip.

"Okay. You know about that. I didn't see it at first, the way Morrie's been getting closer and closer to the edge with these so-called jokes. This time . . . Lars couldn't have done it. Morrie had to have signed me in at Forest House; he'd done something sort of similar before."

The fat-farm incident.

"My brother had me committed while I was out cold," Manny said. His voice was flat and unemotional. Deliberately so, I thought.

"How did it happen?"

"I was getting ready to go to Oaxaca. The pressure was on; I knew the phony evidence suggesting the existence of *The Silver King* wouldn't hold up under scrutiny. There wouldn't have been any other way to keep a lid on the Stevenson thing if I didn't hide out."

"I still don't altogether understand your Stevenson caper," I said. "But you can tell me more about it later."

"As I said, I was going to go away. Only I had an appointment with my masseur first; he always comes to the house on Mondays." He shook his head. "I should have known better, after what happened on the Fourth of July." Manny looked up at me, pain and sorrow evident on his face. "Morrie invited me to his place for a barbecue. Then he tried to get me drunk." He looked away from me, out across the balcony, and was silent for a while. "Anyway, I wasn't suspicious when I got the phone call that Monday morning. It was some guy I didn't know. My regular masseur couldn't come and this other fellow said he'd do it."

"Someone Morrie sent?" I asked.

"You got it." Manny's voice was flatter than ever, his mouth a grim line.

"And the replacement was Lars Hanson?"

"Lars Hanson in disguise. Weirdest-looking getup I ever saw. I should have known right then."

I said nothing, waiting for him to continue.

"Lars thought I wouldn't recognize him when I saw him later at Forest House. He works there; that's where he is now. The man's an egomaniac, I suppose. As well as a few other things."

Manny didn't continue. After a while, I asked a question

to get him going again. "What kind of disguise did Lars wear?"

"A weird getup, like I said. A fake beard, and he'd done something to darken his skin. He had on a bandanna, and one gold earring."

"The operetta hippie!"

"Yeah. You could put that name to the way he looked."

"Does Lars have a motorcycle?"

Manny looked at me, startled. "Yes. One of those old Harley Electraglides." He favored me with a wry grin. "You must be one of those people who knows everything."

"If I was so smart I wouldn't be where I am right now."

He grunted in agreement. "I saw Lars in costume, but minus the beard," I told Manny. "He came to Valley Savings while the sketch of you was on display. Frannie and I were going to follow him, but he left on his bike almost before we were out of the bank." I thought again of Lars's towering anger, his fierce breathing. "He was pretty upset about that picture."

Manny chuckled. "He was royally pissed."

Even strong language, I thought, didn't do justice to the man's rage.

"Lars goes out in that stupid disguise sometimes," Manny said. "Whenever he does, he uses the motorcycle."

G. Gordon Liddy stuff, I thought. Disguises and derring-do. But Lars was someone to be taken very seriously.

"I still don't understand about you being in Forest House," I said after a while, "or why the sketch was in the art show."

"Lars put me in Forest House, at the request of my brother." The flat, controlled-emotion tone of voice had returned. "One minute I was relaxing on the massage table, eyes closed, waiting for this replacement guy to get started. Next thing I know, it's a day later and I'm at Forest House with one hell of a hangover and this knot on the back of my head. My throat hurt, too. The bastard must have used a feeding tube—it's the only way he could have gotten the booze inside me."

"That's . . . bizarre."

"Yeah. But it fits. Remember, Morrie tried to get me drunk earlier, at his Fourth of July bash. I let it go. At the time I thought I'd won a round, evaded one of his jokes. I never thought Morrie would . . ." He shook his head.

I waited before I asked my next question. "The sketch, why did you pose for it?"

"Ah, yes. The sketch." Manny shifted position, and sat with his back resting against the wall. "I thought then it was going to be a joke—my lighthearted bid for attention, my ticket to freedom, the way to catch up my brother in a trap of his own making." He sighed. "The perfect game plan. Theresa would enter the sketch in the show, our friends would see it, and, voilà, everyone would start asking questions. People would realize I hadn't gone on a vacation after all. Morrie would be finessed, have to let me out, and I'd have won the round."

"But how would the people who saw the sketch at the bank know that it had been made so recently? There wasn't any date on it."

Manny sighed. "I didn't think of that at the time or I would have asked Theresa to date the sketch," he said. "I guess I was still a little out of it."

Small wonder, I thought, considering what he'd been through. I didn't want to dwell on the subject. "Morrie had the sketch withdrawn from the show," I said.

"That would be just like him."

"He was fooled by the signature on the picture, just the way my friend and I were. He decided to get Adrianna out of town—showed up at her house pretending to be selling tickets in a church raffle, and saw to it that she won a trip to Hawaii."

"*He* did it? Morrie went to this woman's house himself?"

"Absolutely. And he wanted to disguise himself, so he was wearing a toupée."

Manny exploded with laughter, and sat rocking back and forth. "Morrie . . . wearing a rug," he managed at last, still chuckling. "That's rich."

"How well did you know Theresa Simoni?" I asked, sorry to be going back to a somber topic when this was probably the first laugh he'd had since he'd come here.

"Theresa?" The laughter was gone. "I got to know her while I was in Forest House. They had this art therapy class and I spotted her stuff. She was good, a professional. Nice woman, too."

"And?"

"She was going home that weekend. I told her I wanted a sketch and wanted her to enter it in the art show. She promised. So I posed for the class, told her I'd send her a check when I got out, and we were in business."

"You won't have to send her the check."

"No." He was silent, contemplative.

"From what we learned in the neighborhood," I said, "Lars spent some time there asking questions about Adrianna and Theresa."

"Why would he do that?"

"I don't know. I thought maybe you would."

"I don't."

"How do you think Lars knew the picture was in the bank?"

"Morrie told him, I suppose."

"He must have noticed the signature on the sketch, just like I did. And apparently he found out that Adrianna was Theresa's daughter."

"He must have been pissed at Theresa, too."

I didn't answer right away. "Obviously," I said finally.

Morrie sighed. "What did Lars do to Theresa?"

I didn't want to tell him Lars had gotten Theresa drunk. "Her body was found in the river. She had been struck on the back of the head."

Manny put his head down on his arms. I decided it was time to take a break from the conversation. I moved out on to the balcony.

The spot must have been delightful once—flooded with sunshine in the winter, shaded in the summer by the wisteria that had been planted by the base of the pergola. But now the vines afforded no greenery; they were gaunt skeletons clinging to the pergola's timbers. Wisteria would be dormant this time of year, in any event, but the dried, gray tendrils didn't look like this past summer's growth. They were old, from a long-ago season when someone here had watered the big planter boxes through the hot, dry summer.

In the center of the balcony area, beyond reach, stood an uneven row of red-and-white checkered food containers. Flies and yellowjackets swarmed around them. Trails of ants led to the cartons, and also to the scattered contents of the container Lars had kicked yesterday. In the balcony corner more flies buzzed around a puddle, and a small pile of excrement—further evidence of Lars's talent for humiliation.

I moved back inside. "Lars is at work at Forest House?" I asked.

"Yep. He's taken great pains to explain to me that no one will suspect him because he's still holding down his job."

"He works a swing shift?"

Manny nodded. "Wednesday through Sunday."

Today was Wednesday.

"You missed the fun, his two days off." Manny ran a hand through his hair. "I've had it up to here with his *reasonable man* crap."

"I can well imagine."

"I tried to get him off my back on Monday. It didn't work."

"What happened?"

"I hinted around that he should check out the round barn in Santa Rosa. It's the only building remaining in the old Fountaingrove colony. You know that part of the story?"

I said I did.

"I felt like I had to tell him something. But it was a mistake. There was a chain-link fence and a security guard there, and the damn place was swarming with people. Lars came back madder than a hornet."

Manny looked off into the distance, his mouth a grim line. I wondered what Lars had done in retaliation. Manny bore no bruises that I could see, but Lars would know how to inflict pain without leaving marks.

He sighed. "I should never have started this Stevenson stunt. It's out of hand—it's like what happened with the sorcerer's apprentice."

I remembered the story. The old folk tale was used as a segment of the Walt Disney movie *Fantasia*. The sorcerer's apprentice tired of bringing buckets of water into the castle. While the master was away, the apprentice imitated his magic to bring a broom to life, and he commanded it to fetch water. But he didn't know how to make the broom stop; by the time the Sorcerer returned, the castle was flooded and the poor apprentice was in major trouble.

Manny stirred restlessly. "I think maybe the same thing's happened to Morrie."

"You mean, you believe Lars has gone a whole lot further than your brother intended—that if he knew what was going on here, he wouldn't want it that way?"

Manny got up and began to pace. "There have been phone calls; I think they're from Morrie. Lars goes downstairs to take them, so I haven't heard much—not the exact words; my hearing's not what it used to be. But I could catch the tone of it, I know they argued. It was the same every call. First the arguing, then Lars being persuasive, trying to talk my brother out of something—coming here, I suppose." Manny stopped his pacing and again ran a hand through his hair, weariness evident in the nervous gesture. "I keep telling myself Morrie doesn't want it this way, that Lars is in it for himself now."

"I'm sorry about your brother," I said after a while. "Even if he's only partly responsible."

Manny sat down again. "I've been sorry about him for a long time."

After a while I stood up and went over to stand in the doorway.

"Now I don't know what's going on," Manny said, his voice tight with apprehension. "Morrie hasn't called for a couple of days."

I could find no words of reassurance for him.

I stood in silence, staring out at the grassy ridgetop across the ravine and considering our situation. I had no idea how we'd make it out of this. Manny couldn't gain our freedom by giving Lars what he wanted, because *The Silver King* didn't exist. And should Lars discover the hoax, he'd kill us without a moment's hesitation.

The thought wasn't conducive to sleeping, nor was the bare, cold hardwood floor. I finally dozed off, only to be awakened in the middle of the night by the rattle of a diesel engine. I sat up and listened to the sounds of Lars's return; Manny, too, had awakened and was sitting up.

We heard the garage door rumble open, the Mercedes pull in. There was a long silence before the garage door closed— Lars must have been out there with a flashlight, I thought, sweeping away tire prints. Then there were more sounds: a door opening and closing down below, footsteps on the stairs. When Lars snapped on the light Manny and I blinked in the unaccustomed brightness.

He held up two containers of french fries. "Dinner," he announced in a mockingly sweet voice. He turned the bags over, scattering the fries on the floor.

I stared at the cold, greasy food, stuck with gobbets of congealed fat. Saliva formed in my mouth until I had to swallow.

Humiliation. Lars was good at it.

He laughed, then turned off the light and left. Manny and I moved to the center of the room and started groping in the dim light for our food.

"He'll leave us alone now," Manny said. "He wants to get his beauty sleep so he can give us his full attention in the morning."

$\triangledown$

22

Lᴀʀs, ᴏʙɴᴏxɪᴏᴜsʟʏ ᴄʜᴇᴇʀFᴜʟ, ᴘᴜᴛ in an early appearance the next morning. He'd brought a mug of coffee upstairs with him, and made much of strolling out on to the balcony to enjoy the morning air. He took a long pull at the mug. "Ah!" he exclaimed, smacking his lips with exaggerated satisfaction.

I could see steam rising from the coffee, smell its fragrance. I turned my head away and tried not to salivate.

"Bastard!" Manny muttered sotto voce.

Lars, pacing back and forth, began another soliloquy. Manny stared stolidly into the distance; I emulated him and did my best to ignore Lars's ranting.

I watched the man idly, trying to take his measure. He was cold and ruthless, of that I had no doubt. And intelligent. Also totally committed to what he was doing—he never flagged, never skipped a detail.

I found myself wondering what he would do if the real estate agent brought someone here to look at the place. To anyone who merely drove up the driveway and inspected the house from the outside it would seem unoccupied. But the realtor would have a lockbox key and would come inside.

I had no doubt Lars would kill with chilling efficiency anyone who came here. I envisioned him waiting just inside the front door, blackjack in hand. It would be the blackjack, not the rifle, I was sure of that. The weapon was quiet, probably untraceable. And Lars was expert in using it. Manny had told me he'd bragged repeatedly about his ability to inflict exactly the injury he desired.

Lars was still talking, explaining now in great detail the delicious food and drink that could be ours if only Manny would be reasonable. I listened briefly, then pushed his voice out of my awareness so that I could think my own thoughts.

Today was Thursday. Lars had captured me on Tuesday, *presented* me to Manny yesterday. Two days had gone by, two days during which I was supposedly working in Oakland. Frannie wouldn't know I was missing, nor the McAdoos—for the umpteenth time I wished I hadn't gotten nettled and left that phone message saying they might not see me until later in the week. But surely by now they'd be wondering where I was. Maybe they'd phone Frannie; I'd given them her number. But they might not have been able to reach her; Mike had her all wrapped up in his search for the nonexistent Stevenson book. *Damn!* But Frannie would be expecting me home sometime tonight. And by tomorrow morning at the latest she would realize I was missing and tell Vince, who'd be worried out of his skin.

Then what?

I tried to think through possible ways they could know I was here. I hadn't written Julie's name on our list of possible leads, but Frannie had to think of talking to her eventually, I told myself. I shook my head, regretting my assurances to Julie that Morrie couldn't possibly have kidnapped Manny. I realized I'd done a thorough job on myself all the way down the line—telling the McAdoos they could cool their heels, not letting anyone know where I was going, convincing Julie her kidnapping theory was full of holes.

Lars had paused in his spiel. I looked up to see him leaning back on the pergola; he smiled evilly at me and made much of enjoying the last of his coffee. I stared back at him blankly, my mind still halfway lost in my own thoughts—until I realized that, behind him, standing on the top of the ridge beyond, were two men. I blinked, scarcely believing my eyes.

The two were in plain sight, apparently having followed the same route to the ridgetop as I had. One was tall and slender and the other short and rotund. Mike's Japanese Mutt and Jeff. I wanted to scream: *Duck down!*

I closed my eyes momentarily, willing them to have the sense to get out of sight. I opened my eyes; they were still up there in plain view. The tall one pulled out a pair of binoculars and began studying the house. Too late, I realized that Lars was looking at me intently, reading my expression. He whirled, following my gaze, and saw the two Japanese.

"Shit!"

An instant later Lars was inside the house. He wrenched the automatic rifle from its rack and came back outside. He took aim, fired. The weapon made a deafening noise, setting my ears ringing. The shorter of the two Japanese fell instantly, while the tall one started to run in great, desperate bounds down the spine of the ridge. Lars opened fire again. The deafening sound continued mercilessly. I watched, dazed. For one brief moment I thought the man might make it. But then, arms and legs flailing, he fell to the ground.

Lars, seemingly unaffected by the blast of sound from the automatic rifle, moved with incredible speed to replace it on its rack. Then he ran down the stairs.

I shook my head, the noise still sounding in my ears. Manny had gone out onto the balcony; I followed, stretching my tether to move as near to the far edge as I could.

Lars, shovel in hand, soon came into our line of view, heading for the ravine. After a few moments he emerged on the far side, without the shovel, and climbed the slope beyond. We watched as he hauled one body and then the other down into the ravine. I knew exactly what he was planning to do. The ground was too hard anywhere else; he'd bury them in the dry pond. There was sure to be a deep accumulation of sand and gravel there—and not only would it be easy to dig but all traces of the burial would soon be under-water. The winter rains would start the creek flowing again by December, maybe sooner.

There was nothing more to see. Manny and I went back inside and sat together in stunned silence. Hours later Lars returned to the house. We could hear him moving about down below, showering, readying himself to go to work. Then he came upstairs. Without a word to us, he filled the dog food bowl with water and left.

Manny and I still did not talk. Finally, as darkness fell, I curled up in the back corner of the room in a futile effort to go to sleep.

I was miserable, numb, still half-deaf. Nonetheless, I tried to think what had happened, how the two Japanese had found Hummingbird House. Sheer persistence, I supposed. They'd been all over the Napa Valley, checking out every-thing, and had even gotten themselves arrested for trespass-ing. My mind was working slowly and wouldn't make the details fit neatly together, but somehow I felt they must have found the place because they'd been following Myrna Pur-cell. She was trying to sell information to Morrie, apparently, and was having trouble getting in touch with him. So why wouldn't she have checked into the Wulff family, found out about Julie, and tracked her down somehow? Or, I specu-lated, maybe she thought Julie would pay for information.

That idea was so laughable I struggled to hold back a fit of the giggles, which I did by turning my mind to something simpler: the task of remembering the names of the two Jap-anese men. Try as I might, I could recall only that Mike had said the tall one called himself Slim, and pronounced it "Srim." With that, I started to cry.

I made no effort to stop the tears that slid out of my eyes and down my cheeks but instead moved so that my arm would be under my face and the tears could be soaked up by my shirtsleeve. Eventually, I was able to go to sleep.

▽

23

I SLEPT FITFULLY, SHIFTING position repeatedly on the cold floor. Finally, I sat up. Manny was awake, too; I could just make out his silhouette. He was sitting with his arms around his knees, facing the sliding glass door.

I went over to sit beside him. I felt the need to talk, but not about what had happened today. It was too recent, too dreadful—a demon to be exorcised with talk of something else. "How did you get from Forest House to here?" I asked.

"Exactly the same way I got there—a bash on the head, another hangover, another sore throat."

I thought about what must have happened, grateful to have the task to occupy my mind. Lars must have seen to it that Manny was passed out cold, and probably also left evidence indicating Manny had smuggled liquor in to Forest House. Then he'd have reported the incident to the people in charge, who would, of course, summon Morrie. And Morrie would declare he was taking Manny elsewhere. I imagined Morrie feigning unhappiness about his "incorrigible" brother. Or maybe he would pretend to be outraged and say he couldn't leave Manny in such a lax treatment facility. However it worked, Morrie had not only assented

but had been part of the act. And, of course, he was the one
who knew about Hummingbird House. They must have
simply broken in, confident that the real estate agent would
be none the wiser.

The only missing ingredient was Morrie's motivation.

Still grateful for the distraction, I pursued that line of
thinking. There was the long-standing rivalry, of course, the
exchange of pranks. But just recently something that had
gone on for years had taken on a much more hostile bent. I
tried to piece together from my limited information what
might have changed in Morrie's life. Two things I knew of:
his father had recently died and, after that, he and Julie had
separated. Maybe Morrie at last felt free of parental control;
maybe he thought his wife had been having an affair with
Manny; maybe both factors were operating.

None of these thoughts led to good conversational fodder,
but it didn't seem to matter. We sat in companionable silence. There was a full moon out; the balcony looked pleasant and unsullied. I felt soothed but not yet ready to deal
with the killing we'd witnessed.

"How did you get started on the Stevenson thing?" I asked
after a while.

"The Silverado Museum has pestered me for donations
from time to time over the years. Usually I wrote a check,
the same amount I give any charity. But I didn't think much
about contributing a substantial amount—at least not until
after something that happened on my birthday."

The fat-farm caper, I thought.

"I got to thinking about things and the whole Stevenson
idea just landed in my lap. I knew it would be a great joke
to play on Morrie."

"So what did you do?"

"I gave the people at the Silverado Museum a bunch of
money and told them I would probably be doing research at
the museum from time to time. Then I let on to Morrie that
I was interested in Stevenson. Not directly, but by buying
Stevenson stuff, first editions and the like, and leaving it

around when he came over. I also put my name out at a lot of places that deal in books and antiques. I go off on these tangents; it wasn't hard to convince Morrie that this was my latest thing."

The documents I'd seen had looked authentic; I wondered how he'd done it. "You created some documents to make everybody believe there was a *Silver King* manuscript? How did you do that?"

"I went out and hired a forger, as simple as that."

He grinned at me. "I was really into it by then, having a hell of a good time. I knew I'd have to have an accomplice, someone who could not only forge the documents but pretend to discover them."

"So what did you do?" I asked. "I mean to find your forger?"

"I went over to the Sonoma State campus, hung around the student exchange drinking coffee and talking to students. I concentrated on the ones old enough to be graduate students, chatted them up. It wasn't long before I found what I needed—a woman with some training in historical research who had a very large need for money. After that it was easy." He chuckled. "We didn't have to accomplish a complete forgery. There were a couple of old documents that turned up; all she had to do was add a bit to them."

So that was why the "Dear Charles" letter had looked so authentic. It was, except for the added-on handwriting.

Manny sighed. "I was astonished it was so easy."

Easy, I thought, except he never anticipated the furor that would be generated and the attention that would be focused on the documents. Inevitably it would come to light that the additions weren't authentic.

"Why did this graduate student want the money?"

"She was planning on an acting career but she was in an accident." The same story Helen Chaffee had told me. Nonetheless, I let him tell it from beginning to end. "In the meantime," Manny concluded, "while she was waiting for the lawsuit to be settled, she signed up as a graduate student in history—history of the theater."

The temptation was too much to resist. "I gaze into my crystal ball," I said, affecting a fortune teller's style. "The woman's last name is Purcell."

Manny fell into the mood with me. "Not again!" he said, putting a hand to his forehead in mock dismay.

I told him how I knew, that I'd spotted Myrna at the Silverado Museum. "She acted like a stock Mysterious Character, I called her Ms. Floppy Hat."

Manny threw back his head and laughed.

I asked Manny if he could think of a reason Myrna might have been seeking out his brother. "She spent a lot of time trying to get in touch with him. Why would she be doing that?"

"I don't know. Money, probably. She must have known he was after *The Silver King.*"

That seemed plausible. "Do you think Mryna would continue the scam on her own? I mean, play both ends against the middle and hit your brother up for money?"

"Sure. That's why she agreed to work for me. I think she'd do anything for money."

The sorcerer's apprentice bit all over again, I thought. "Did she know you were supposed to be going away on vacation?" I asked.

"Everybody knew," Manny said glumly. "I was taking pains to make sure Morrie knew, trying to get him to think I'd lost interest in the Stevenson thing."

"But at that point the idea was too powerful," I said. "Everyone was stirred up. Myrna, news reporters, treasure seekers."

"Yeah."

No need to rub it in. Manny had gotten more than he'd bargained for. All around. "Another thing," I said. "You went to that place in San Francisco—The Argonaut—and bought things related to a woman who had been at Fountaingrove. Why did you do that?"

Manny treated me to a grin. "I thought you knew everything."

"Almost," I said, "but not quite."

"Strictly window dressing," Manny said. "Or maybe there'd be something Myrna and I could use if she needed more evidence." He paused, seeming lost in thought. "You know," he went on, "at the outset it looked like so much fun. I knew Morrie would fall for it. And the best part was going to be that he'd have only himself to blame when he found out he had egg on his face. If he weren't so all-fired eager to keep up with me, he wouldn't have been suckered into it."

"How did all this get started between you?"

Manny shifted, sat up a little straighter, turned slightly toward me. "It goes a long way back. Between the two of us, I was always the one to step out first. When we were kids, it never caused any problems. It was just the way things were. But then Morrie really blew a gasket about the birthday party. Our eighteenth. That was back when we were still living in the old house out at the ranch. My mother was planning to go all out in style for this one."

I caught a note of enthusiasm for the telling of the story in his voice, a trace of the raconteur.

"They hired a caterer, some musicians." He shook his head. "I thought about it not long ago."

Vengeance, I thought. Maybe Morrie had never forgiven the Jell-O caper. It's always seemed to me that taking vengeance wreaks more havoc on the avenger than anyone else.

Manny had paused, seeming as lost in his own thoughts as I was in mine, but now he continued. "There was a slew of kids invited to that party. Family friends, too. I really shouldn't have done what I did. But the idea was too much fun to resist. And my mother was kind of stuffy—maybe I was rebelling against that."

Soon he was back into the telling of the story, with relish. I didn't tell him I already knew it; I wouldn't have spoiled his fun for anything. And when he finished, he stood up, stretching. He yawned.

"Time for some sleep at last," I ventured.

He regarded me somberly for a moment, as if considering whether to talk about what had kept us awake. No need, I thought, not now. "Good night," I said, and moved back to the same corner.

Some time later, just before I went to sleep, I remembered the names of the two Japanese men. Biff Okada and Slim Takehara.

▽

24

Lᴀʀs ʜᴀᴅ ʙʀᴏᴜɢʜᴛ ᴜs no food the night before. But the next morning, Friday, he brought in two cartons of cottage cheese. Just cottage cheese—no frills and extras such as spoons. He filled the dog food bowl and went back downstairs without having said a word. At least, I thought, he hadn't dumped our food on the floor.

As soon as he had left, Manny took the cartons over to the sliding glass doors, where the first thin strands of autumn sunlight had begun to illuminate the balcony. He made a mock bow. "Breakfast on the patio," he said. He took the lid off one of the cottage cheese cartons, bent it, and handed it to me with a flourish. "Your spoon, m'dear."

I marveled at his attempt to keep up our spirits, to make the best of adversity. The bent cottage cheese lid was uncomfortably flat and wide; I had to stretch my mouth to accommodate it. And I tried to stretch my mood, too, momentarily to forget yesterday and go along with the spirit Manny had established.

"This works fine," I said, gesturing with the cottage cheese lid, "as long as I remember to keep smiling."

I felt enormously rewarded with the grin he flashed at me.

But our tête-à-tête didn't last long. We heard a car motor and tires scrunching on the gravel of the turnaround area. We hurried to look out the front windows. A late-model Honda stood in the turnaround area. It had a rental agency sticker on the back bumper. By now Lars had opened the garage door and was climbing behind the wheel of the Honda.

"What in the hell?" Manny muttered.

Lars started the car and pulled it in to the garage alongside my old Dodge truck.

"The car must have belonged to those two Japanese guys," I said. I was surprised, now that I came to think of it, that Lars had left it out on the road overnight. "I guess he didn't have time to bring it in yesterday," I surmised aloud.

Manny said nothing but only turned and went back to where he usually sat, facing the balcony from the open doorway.

I paced the room restlessly, wanting a serious talk with Manny. With what had happened yesterday, I'd begun to consider how much longer we had before the whole situation exploded. But I was nervous that Lars, with his snoopy habits, might overhear. Finally I decided to risk a quiet conversation, and went to sit beside Manny. I made several starts at getting around to talking about yesterday's killings. I figured we needed to get the subject out in the open first, clear the air. But Manny resisted. He'd look away, shake his head, then begin talking about something else. I began to reconsider our breakfast on the patio—whether it had been a brave effort at gallantry or a dangerous retreat from reality.

Manny, taking over the conversation, embarked on a soliloquy about his relationship with Morrie.

"Never in my life did I ask my brother to compete with me. I just did things I wanted to do, followed my interests. But Morrie took it as a challenge every time. He was always trying to keep up with me, always one step behind."

I thought fleetingly about the odd little woman I'd seen at Valley Savings, with her cream-colored jogging suit and coordinated hosiery and mid-heel pumps—one step behind all her life.

"Maybe," Manny went on, "I should have turned around and extended a helping hand, invited him to share what I was doing. But damnit! I resented his constant imitation of me. What do the kids say? *Get a life.*"

His vehemence surprised me.

"I tried to ignore Morrie's mean streak. I kept thinking . . . hell!" Manny lapsed into silence, then abruptly began speaking again. "I wasn't smart enough to see that the things he'd started doing were a change, that they weren't just new episodes in the same old game."

"You couldn't change Morrie," I said. "It wasn't your fault." And Morrie isn't the one we should be worrying about, I added, to myself.

Lars came up the stairs at that point, bringing a steaming mug of coffee. He began pacing up and down the room, giving us the same old line of palaver. He stopped after a while and deliberately leaned back against the wall by the bathroom door, his shoulder close to—almost touching—the automatic rifle.

"Your Japanese friends," he said in a mocking voice, "were not very smart."

We remained silent. Lars could have no way of knowing who they were—he had to be fishing for information.

"When next any of your friends come calling," Lars went on, "we must be more polite." He scanned Manny's face, then mine. "Perhaps we'll invite them in for tea?" Lars crossed his arms and leaned back, almost snuggling against the terrible weapon.

Manny sat and stared fixedly at nothing. I looked stolidly away, with an effort keeping the sights and sounds of yesterday's killings from my mind.

I was momentarily pleased with my success at making my mind a blank, with my capacity to make Lars's words fade to a meaningless jumble. And then it hit me, what Manny was doing—what *I* was doing! Dear God! We'd learned to *endure* all too well.

Manny's lethargy was understandable, given what he'd been through. But mine was not.

Think! Get us out of this—you're the only one who can.

Lars was thoroughly effective at keeping us incarcerated; there was no getting around that. We couldn't undo our shackles—we'd tried often enough. And I could think of no way we could signal for help. In any event, a rescue attempt from outside, unless Lars was away at work, would lead to disaster. But there had to be something we hadn't yet thought of. I watched Lars as he again paced back and forth, *declaiming*. By now he must be feeling extraordinarily frustrated; surely he'd lose patience before long.

I was startled by the ringing of the telephone.

Lars went downstairs to take the call.

I leaned forward, straining to hear. "So you're back." Lars's voice was flat. Almost hostile, I thought. "Absolutely not," he said, his voice tinged with contempt. "We can't accomplish anything by that. Do what I tell you. Let me handle this." Then Lars hung up—I could hear him bang down the receiver. But he did not come back up the stairs.

Manny said nothing, but went to sit in the open doorway to the balcony. I paced the room for a while, then went to gaze out the front window, staring unseeingly at the turnaround area below. Escape seemed impossible yet imperative—we'd have to do it somehow. Perhaps today, after Lars left for work. But we had virtually no resources, only the clothes on our backs. I mentally inventoried my wardrobe. I didn't even have my belt; Lars had taken it. And he'd emptied my pockets before he'd put me in that storage room.

My eyeglasses. I drew in my breath with the suddenness of the thought. How could I have been so paralyzed that I hadn't thought of it sooner?

We could collect dry leaves and start a fire on the balcony. All we would need was a good plume of smoke. In these tinder-dry hills, the Department of Forestry fire trucks would be here in no time. No, the start-with-a-lens trick was the stuff of the Saturday afternoon serials I'd watched when I was a youngster. I had a sinking feeling this kind of stuff worked only in the movies.

What else could I do with my eyeglasses?

Break a lens.

It was so simple. I froze with excitement, still staring out the front windows. As soon as Lars left, we'd smash one lens and use a shard of glass to cut the nylon tethers. Maybe, I thought, my spirits soaring, Lars left the keys to my truck in the ignition.

Below, Vince's Chevy emerged from the shade of the ravine and pulled to a stop. Almost unbelieving, I watched Vince open his car door, get partway out and stand beside the car. After a moment, Frannie got out of the passenger side.

Lars had to know Vince and Frannie were out there, had to have heard them, seen them. Go away, I pleaded silently, directing all my emotional energy into transmitting the thought. Just go away. I didn't want them to see anything to alert them that we were here, didn't want them to notice the sterile, swept-clean gravel.

Frannie took a few uncertain steps toward the front entrance, then stopped and stood looking up at the house. I continued to stare, still half-disbelieving, and at the same time remembered when I had first come here. I'd stood on that very spot. I'd looked up at the dusty upstairs windowpanes; they'd stared back, blankly reflecting the sun's glare. I'd thought the house uninhabited then. Please think so, too, Frannie.

Vince and Frannie couldn't have stood in the turnaround area for more than a few minutes. It seemed an eternity. Endless moments passed while I willed the two of them not to see anything out of place, not to imagine that we might be behind the blind stare of those dusty windows. Finally, Vince shook his head, said something to Frannie. She got back in the car; he turned it around. And then the old Chevy disappeared into the shade of the driveway.

An instant later Lars bounded up the stairs. "Your friends

are very lucky," he told us, sneering, and disappeared back down the stairs.

I ignored him, my mind filled with thoughts for Vince's and Frannie's safety, with new schemes for escape. I was eager to tell my plans to Manny, to make him listen, bring him back to life and get him to take part. But I didn't dare say a word yet, for fear Lars would overhear—no matter that he'd gone back downstairs.

Before long Lars returned and went into the bathroom. He emerged with a low stool, which he placed in the center of the room.

Dear Lord! What now?

He went back into the bathroom and turned on the water in the basin. I looked at Manny in inquiry. He sat as if frozen, his face deadly pale. I turned back. Lars, at the bathroom basin, was running water over a large bath towel. I watched, fascinated; the muscles in his arms bulged as he wrung it out. I felt suddenly weak. Lars planned to work Manny over, right in front of my eyes.

Lars finished with the towel. He brought it into the room and made a great ceremony of folding it and placing it on the stool. All the while he kept his gaze on me, judging my reaction, I thought. Unwilling to give him any satisfaction, I stared boldly back. He picked up one of the towels, smiling maliciously. And moved toward me.

Someone pounded on the front door.

Lars, cursing, flung down the towel but made no move to leave the room. I hurried to the window, Manny only a step behind me. In the yard below was a Jaguar, the cloud of dust caused by its precipitous arrival still settling.

"Christ!" Manny said. "That's Morrie's car."

I heard the front door opening and Morrie shouting for Lars as he moved from room to room downstairs. Then he started up the stairs, still calling out for Lars.

After that, everything happened with incredible speed. Lars darted to the wall, took the blackjack from its peg, and positioned himself alongside the top of the stairs. Almost at the same instant, Morrie emerged from the stairwell. "No!" Manny shouted. "Stay away!" I warned. But Lars moved with a terrible swiftness, catching Morrie on the back of the head with the blackjack.

Morrie sank silently to the floor. Manny, crying with anguish, struggled furiously against his tether. Lars stepped quickly into the bathroom and emerged with a dry towel, which he tucked under Morrie's head. Then he stooped over the unconscious man and applied two cruel, fierce, skull-crushing blows.

I turned away, but not soon enough. I saw the blood start, a terrible red stain spreading swiftly through the white terry cloth beneath Morrie's head.

Manny sobbed relentlessly. I stood—I don't know how long—head in hands, seeing over and over those swift, cruel blows, the spreading red stain. Eventually, Manny's sobs subsided and I found the strength to take my hands away from my eyes.

Lars stood in the entry to the bathroom, leaning casually against the door frame. In one hand he held a washcloth, in the other his blackjack. With meticulous care, he was cleaning it of every trace of blood.

25

T HE LIGHTS WENT OFF. Lars, startled, looked around, his glance darting rapidly here and there as if to discover what had caused the disruption.

The phone rang.

Lars, thoroughly alarmed now, stared at it, then picked it up gingerly, listened. An instant later he hurled it away as if it were a live rattlesnake, snatched the rifle from the rack, and ran down the stairs.

Outside, a microphone-amplified voice began speaking, announcing that the house was surrounded.

We had been rescued.

How? My mind raced with possibilities—the likeliest being that Vince, or maybe Frannie, had noticed the swept-clean parking area and come to the same conclusion that I had.

I jumped up and stared out the front windows. I could just barely see the front of a patrol car in the shade of the driveway—both front doors were open like wings, gun barrels poking around the sides. I imagined somewhere, farther back, behind all the law enforcement people, Vince in his car, waiting, anxious and impatient.

The microphone voice continued. The house was surrounded, we were reminded. We should throw out our weap-

ons and come out on our hands and knees. The instructions
were repeated several times, and then a second voice took
over the microphone, a gentler one. "Morrie Wulff, please
listen to me, I want to talk to you."

Dear Lord! I glanced at Manny. He sat impassive.

If they thought Morrie was our captor, they must have
talked with Julie. Or, rather, Vince and Frannie had to have
located us through her. Of course! They'd realized I was
missing, talked to Julie, then come to the house. Vince must
have called for help right away.

The gentle, pleading voice continued, appealing to
Morrie's better nature, asking him to give himself up, arguing that he had no other course. "Just come out and talk
to us, Morrie. You'll be safe if you surrender."

He went on and on until I was ready to scream, but Manny
gave no sign, no response to the endless repetition of his
brother's name. He sat motionless except for a slight rocking
motion, his arms clasping his knees, his eyes blank.

From somewhere out back came a burst of gunshots, then
another.

I ran to the balcony. Shouts came from the creek; two
officers scurried toward it. With the driveway blocked by
police cars, Lars would have tried to escape by making his
way down the ravine. Now, I assumed, he'd been either captured or killed.

I went to sit beside Manny. "It's over," I said.

He did not respond. The gentle-voiced man pleaded with
us over the microphone to surrender any weapons and come
out of the house on our hands and knees.

"We'll have to wait until our rescuers come inside," I said,
as much to myself as to Manny. I needn't have said anything.
Manny stared straight ahead, seemingly oblivious to everything that was happening.

I got up and looked from the balcony toward the ravine. I
heard faint voices there, or imagined I did, and sounds that
could have been people moving about under the trees. Were
they bringing out Lars's body? Or escorting him out in hand-

cuffs? Maybe he was alive, had eluded them. I shuddered at the possibility—Lars could conceivably have fled from the ravine back into the house!

I told myself to stop inventing remote possibilities, and came back to sit again beside Manny. The voice on the microphone continued to plead, to repeat Morrie's name until I wanted to scream: Stop! Stop! Stop! Stop!

The phone rang again. Manny and I both flinched, startled. "Morrie Wulff," the microphone voice from outside pleaded, "please pick up the telephone and talk with us."

"Shit," Manny muttered.

Glad to hear him say *anything* I reached over and put a reassuring hand on his knee. "It's over," I said again.

But everything seemed to take forever. I listened to the sounds downstairs as the sheriff's team secured the house, room by room. And I'd shouted to tell them to come up the stairs, that we were the only ones here. No matter. The sheriff's men did what the rule book said they were to do, and we had no recourse but to wait.

Finally, our rescuers made their way up the stairs, military style. Once they were actually in the room, they rushed to check the bathroom and the balcony, to examine Morrie's body. Only then did they turn their attention to Manny and me. Long before then, I'd given in to the strain. I sat crying unabashedly, a torrent of tears coursing down my cheeks. And Manny, at last rousing from his stupor, put an arm around me and told me everything would be all right.

I was suddenly overcome with the need to tell my rescuers what had happened: who I was, who Manny was, that the dead man was Morrie Wulff, that there was no one else involved other than the man who had fled the house, and who he was. I was talking a mile a minute and couldn't slow down. I told them about the two Japanese, and where to find their bodies. And about Theresa Simoni.

I was babbling, I knew it. I stopped abruptly, and asked what had happened to Lars.

He was dead. "He fired on the officers who asked him to

surrender, ma'am. They returned the fire."

Manny and I were led from the house and down to the turnaround area, then were transported separately to the Napa County Sheriff's headquarters. I was questioned, given food, then allowed to talk on the phone to Frannie. I was astounded at how happy I was to hear her voice; she cried, and asked over and over, "Are you really all right?"

I finally convinced her I was unharmed. "Dirty and disheveled and hungry, and darn scared for a while—but I'm fine now. By the way, Frannie, how did you know where to come looking for me? I didn't put Julie's name on our list of leads to check."

"Gracious! I didn't even look. Those people—the Mc-Adoos—called me Thursday afternoon. That's the first I knew you weren't working down in Oakland. I was terribly frightened." Frannie, it turned out, had called Vince, then Mike. "We sat down to have a council of war, and I suddenly just realized that with all our detecting Julie was the one person we hadn't talked to yet." Frannie paused.

"Mike said she wouldn't know anything, but Vince stuck up for her. So I called Vivian Butler and got her phone number right away."

"And she told you she thought Morrie had kidnapped Manny?"

"She certainly did."

I could well imagine, considering how she'd unloaded on me when I'd gone to see her. And so much for my powers of persuasion—I apparently hadn't been as successful as I'd thought in talking her out of her kidnapping theory.

"I better get off the phone now, Frannie. They've promised me some clean clothes and a shower."

"You'll feel better soon," Frannie assured me. "Oh, yes! They said we could come down to pick you up."

"You and Vince?"

"Vince insisted on coming," Frannie said coyly. "You're going to ride back with him in his car."

"And you'll be down with Mike in his car?"

"Won't that be nice? We'll have a regular convoy to take you home!"

I'd begun to wonder if the Mike and Frannie consortium had gotten frazzled around the edges. But apparently not. Or at least not yet. "That's fine, Frannie. I've got to go now; one of the deputies has brought in some food."

"Okay. Toodle-oo. Oh, I almost forgot. Vince sends his love."

Frannie Edmundson, matchmaker, was still very much in business.

The food that had been brought to me was from a nearby restaurant, but it was already cold. There was a greasy cheeseburger and a milkshake, which I was nonetheless grateful to have. There were also french fries, cold and congealed. I didn't touch the fries.

After I'd eaten, the same deputy brought me a change of clothes, a set of navy blue sweats with a sheriff's department emblem on the front of the sweatshirt. All the while I was showering and dressing, I could hear in my mind fragments of Lars's harangues—the tantalizing promises he'd made of exquisite food, hot showers, clean clothes. "He's dead," I whispered to myself again and again. "It's over."

There was more questioning, first about the details of our captivity, then about the deaths of Theresa Simoni, the two Japanese, and Morrie Wulff. I had to relate the ins and outs of the Stevenson stunt and also explain how I had come to be involved in all this. Finally, I was told we would soon be allowed to leave.

I was ushered into a hallway. Manny was there, wearing the same sort of sweats the sheriff's deputies had provided me. He looked considerably better but still halfway shellshocked—his shoulders drooped, his hair fell lankly across his forehead. I went over and took his hand, and we held hands while a sheriff's deputy explained what would happen next.

"A large number of news reporters are in the downstairs lobby," we were told. "You are free to talk to them if you wish but we are willing to do all we can to protect you from them as you leave this building. We can take you out a back entrance. Your friends have brought vehicles and are waiting there."

I looked briefly at Manny, and then nodded assent for both of us.

The deputy led us along a back hallway and down a long flight of stairs. At the bottom, I could feel a brief draft of fresh, cool air. Up ahead someone had opened a door, I thought, then closed it again. We went around a corner and found ourselves just inside a double glass door, now closed.

A uniformed deputy who stood by the door looked inquiringly at us. "Are you folks ready to move fast?" As soon as we indicated we were, the deputy opened the door and we stepped out into the chill evening.

Vince's Chevy was pulled over to the near edge of a parking area close by. Mike's red Grand Marquis was there, too, and a limousine.

A shout came from our left. "There they are!"

I glanced over my shoulder. Someone had already started running the half-block distance across the parking lot from the building's main entrance. An instant later a horde of reporters appeared, all running in our direction.

"Damn it!" Manny said, and sprinted for the limousine.

I moved just as fast, making for the open passenger door of Vince's dusty old Chevy.

$\triangledown$

26

I DIDN'T TALK TO Manny again until two weeks later. He showed up, quite unexpectedly, while I was in Oakland working on the McAdoo house.

I'd just finished breaking up the cheap plastic paneling that had been in the dining room and had loaded it into my truck. I'd brushed off the dust from my shirt and pants and was sitting on the top step of the front porch to take a breather. I was altogether startled when his battered Saab pulled up to the curb.

Manny came to the porch and sat down beside me. "Your friend Frannie told me where to find you." He'd made no preamble, no comment on my unorthodox occupation, for which I was glad.

He looked infinitely better than when I'd last seen him, at Morrie's funeral. His shoulders again had a self-assured set; the weariness was gone from his posture.

I'd had no chance to talk to him at the funeral, and wouldn't have attempted much of a conversation if I'd had the opportunity. He'd looked too done in.

"I'm sorry about your brother," I said.

"I'm damn sorry about him, too."

We exchanged glances. This was almost a word-for-word

repetition of a conversation we'd already had.

"Maybe there's not much more to say," I offered.

"I keep wanting it to be over and done with, but . . ."

The news furor was still going on over Morrie's death and the other killings—to say nothing of the revelation that there was no lost Stevenson manuscript.

Mike had been a big help. He'd prepared a statement for Frannie and me to issue to the press, which explained our involvement without revealing many of the details, and said we would have nothing further to offer. I gathered from the news reports that Manny's lawyer had done pretty much the same thing.

We were silent for a long while before Manny spoke. "Maybe I'll go ahead and take that vacation."

The idea made sense to me. I'd been glad to get back to my original plans, too. Even—Lord forgive me!—to see the McAdoos again.

Manny leaned back against the corner post of the porch railing. He talked about this and that, mostly the places he'd been in Mexico—Casa Colonial in Oaxaca, the old port town of San Blas, Mayan ruins by the sea at Tulum. He talked with particular fondness about places where tourists did not go, especially in Baja California.

As he sat beside me recounting his Mexican adventures, I studied him, glad to see the changes a few week's respite had made. He was no longer the prisoner who *endured* but again the jaunty, self-assured man of the sketch.

The equation between us had also changed. While we had been prisoners in that upstairs room, we'd made jokes about my botched attempt to play Knight in Shining Armor to his Damsel in Distress. But there'd been an element of truth in that description of our relationship.

No longer. He was again himself: Manny Wulff, lifelong millionaire, confident and very much in charge of any situation.

All the while, as Manny told his tales of Mexican adventures, he seemed to be studying me. And an enigmatic smile came and went, an upturning at the corners of his mouth accompanied by a playful glint in his eyes. Eventually he fell silent; his smile broadened and then broke forth in that well-remembered irrepressible grin.

"I've brought something for you."

He got up, went to his car, and brought back a large, flat parcel tied with string, which he presented to me. I opened it. Inside, of course, was the sketch. I was delighted to see the familiar image again, and grinned back at the grin in the picture.

"It's yours. I want you to have it."

"But—" I started to protest, then changed my mind. "Thank you," I said. I looked at the sketch once more, then carefully redid the wrappings and propped the package against the porch railing.

Manny was still wearing the same mysterious smile, still had the same playful glint in his eye. "How about a trip to Baja?" he said quite suddenly. "We could go together, the two of us."

I stared at him in surprise.

"I'll take you to Cabo San Lucas. To Los Arcos Hotel in La Paz."

After a moment of shocked surprise, I started to think about the merits of his proposition. Images flooded my mind, extrapolations from what he'd been telling me of his travels. I could see us touring the Baja desert in a Range Rover, staying at haciendas where he had connections, exploring ancient, little-known ruins. There'd be exciting things to do, good conversations. Manny would be superb company, I had no doubt of it.

"We could get married in La Paz."

I was dumbfounded.

I tried to gather my wits, foresee a future with Manny realistically. I'd enjoy the travel. I'd have no more money worries. Most of all, the companionship would be delightful. I remembered with sudden fondness the times we'd shared during our captivity—the quiet talks, the wry humor, the emotional closeness. I thought with affection of Manny's habit of running a hand through his salt-and-pepper hair, and of the brown hair of the long-ago young man in the red convertible. I yearned now to reach out and touch those wavy locks.

But Manny would turn my life around, be in charge of me. He was accustomed to making decisions, to having them accepted without question.

There was only one way things could be—whatever we did, it would always be his agenda. *I'll take you to Cabo San Lucas.* It wouldn't occur to him to suggest we mull over the possibilities and jointly decide where to go and what to do. We could talk about not letting it be this way, but there'd always be an imbalance in our relationship. The habits of a lifetime are hard to change. He'd call the shots. It would always be, *I'll take you.*

Gradually my independence would be erased, my friendships eroded, until I was no longer my own woman.

I sensed that it was my strength and independence that appealed to Manny, but marriage to him would mean I'd become a dependent shadow of my former self, an appendage trailing after him as he pursued his interests. I would resent my loss of identity. Manny would resent the change in me, too, feel cheated.

My silence must have been eloquent. Manny's expression now was tinged with surprise and hurt. But he put on the grin again, and, head tilted to the side, asked a one-word question. "Snorkeling?"

I felt myself close to tears. Manny had made a deliberate attempt to keep things light—and this was as close, I thought, as he might ever come to pleading. The word seemed to hang endlessly in the silence between us. I felt sorry for Manny. He hadn't expected to be turned down, wasn't used to it.

I marshaled my thoughts, considering how to explain them to Manny. But I knew I couldn't. "I'm sorry, Manny," I finally managed. "It would never work."

Unable to look at him any longer, I turned my head away, blinking back tears.

Manny said nothing, but stood up and started slowly down the stairs. He stopped when he got to the sidewalk. I knew he was waiting for me to look at him, meet his gaze. I steeled myself, then looked right at him and did my best to smile. At the same time, I realized, I had slowly begun to shake my head.

Manny gave it one last try. He turned, put his hands on his hips, and assumed the pose in the sketch. He looked back over his shoulder and gave me that same *je ne sais* what-the-hell *quoi* grin, then a beckoning tilt of his head, a come-with-me gesture.

I could look at him no longer. Instead, I stared down at the flaking gray paint on the porch steps beneath my feet, until at last I heard him get into his car and drive away. Only then did I raise my head and gaze at the empty space where his car had been.

"It would never work," I said again.

Emma Chezzet
Frannie Edmondson
Vance Valente once suitar ex cop
Mike Channing surf rd
Vivian Holland Butler   3rd wife julie ins
Maxine Wolff   ex Maxine
Nannie Wolff
        McAdoo hows for cleaning sad
Phylles Butterfield ex Holmes Jinks
Ariadne Kraepps sketch of Maxine
Elizabeth   Vivians Cousin
Jean Schmidt   ser lawyer to Maxine + old fr
Ellen Chaffee curator Silverado Museum
Biff Ohara   } pr
Shin Takehara
Birdie Smith   cov up ? as Museum - burned at history
Myara Purcell at Cal   w/b actress
Miriam Voss   Adrianna's Candelody
Elaine Wilson   maga who drove to airport
Theresa Simone   Al's ma
Homer (Bizz) Wilkins cab-messenger
Lars Hanson   Captor

Thomas Harris Lab Brotherhood follow type Foren sanguine
Kanaye Nagasawa 2nd cousin